Perhaps he'd built up an image of Daisy that no actual woman could live up to

The golden-haired child basking in the sunlight of her father's love had grown into an ethereal goddess…who had an ex-husband and a fourteen-year-old daughter and kept goats. And didn't return his phone calls. Nick mulled this over for a while, tried to come up with some plausible reasons she might *not* want to talk to him. He sneezed. Difficult to think while sneezing.

He had lined up some other interviews, which he would do over the next few days. All peripheral to the biography, though. Truman's relationship with Daisy as it reflected in his art was the central theme of the work; Truman was dead, so no one else really mattered but Daisy.

Dear Reader,

I sometimes think that if, in order to become a parent, we had to apply for the job, the world's population would shrink considerably. I was very young when I had my children and, looking back, the only thing I knew at the time was that I wanted to be a mother. Many years later, with two beautiful and much-loved adult children—and a granddaughter—I wouldn't have changed anything. But I still wish I'd been more prepared for the awesome responsibilities ahead.

In *Out of Control*, Daisy and Nick both struggle with the question of what it takes to be a good parent. Nick loves his daughter but is painfully aware of his shortcomings. Daisy, abandoned by her mother and raised by a decidedly offbeat father, wants her own daughter to feel the emotional security she herself never experienced as a child.

These days as I find myself caring for my ninety-year-old mother, I'm reminded of how cyclical the life process is. I hold my mother's hand as we journey out, much as she once held my hand and as I held the hands of my own children. I haven't always been the perfect daughter (just ask my mum!), just as I'm not always the perfect mother (just ask my kids!), so perhaps it's just as well I never had to apply for the roles. But despite the mistakes I've made, the things I wish I'd done differently, I'm immensely grateful that I was given the opportunity. A life filled with love, compassion and a liberal sprinkling of humor is an invaluable ingredient for making it through the rough times.

I hope you enjoy *Out of Control*. I really do like hearing from you and do my best to answer every letter or e-mail. You can reach me at www.janicemacdonald.com or at PMB 101, 136 E. 8th Street, Port Angeles, WA 98362.

All the best,

Janice

OUT OF CONTROL
Janice Macdonald

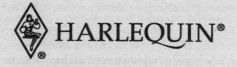

HARLEQUIN®

TORONTO • NEW YORK • LONDON
AMSTERDAM • PARIS • SYDNEY • HAMBURG
STOCKHOLM • ATHENS • TOKYO • MILAN • MADRID
PRAGUE • WARSAW • BUDAPEST • AUCKLAND

ISBN-13: 978-0-373-71378-3
ISBN-10:   0-373-71378-9

OUT OF CONTROL

www.eHarlequin.com

Printed in U.S.A.

ABOUT THE AUTHOR

Janice Macdonald is an author and freelance writer who divides her time between San Diego and Port Angeles, Washington, where she lives in a cabin on the edge of the Olympic National Forest and watches deer graze when she should be writing! She recently discovered the joys of Bach and now listens to his music constantly.

Books by Janice Macdonald

Don't miss any of our special offers. Write to us at the following address for information on our newest releases.

Harlequin Reader Service
U.S.: 3010 Walden Ave., P.O. Box 1325, Buffalo, NY 14269
Canadian: P.O. Box 609, Fort Erie, Ont. L2A 5X3

PROLOGUE

October 6, 2003

Ms. Daisy Fowler
Chaparral Hills
Laguna Beach, California,
U.S.A.

Dear Ms. Fowler:
I am writing to let you know that I have been
contracted to write a biography of your late
father, Mr. Frank Joseph Truman.

I first became interested in your father's work
after seeing a painting in his *Innocence* series
in a London art gallery. The portrait of a young
girl on a sunlit bluff was exquisite; I recall
standing in the wet chill of a November
evening but feeling almost transported. For a
moment, I'd felt the ocean wind that tangled

the girl's hair, tasted the tang of salt on my own lips. My captivation was complete when I learned from the gallery owner that this was a painting of the artist's only daughter.

On a very personal note, having a daughter who is probably a year or so younger than you were when Mr. Truman painted you, I experienced what I can only describe as a connection to and a profound admiration for him as a father. I couldn't help thinking that his love must have contributed to the magical beauty of the work.

I am the author of three previous biographies, most recently, *Antonio Bongiovanni, the Italian Tenor*, scheduled for publication later this year. I am also a frequent contributor to the *London Times*.

I hope you will agree that a well-researched, sympathetic biography of your father would be a tribute to his memory, and, to that end, I would like to schedule a time that we can meet to discuss this project. I will contact you when I arrive in Laguna the first of next month. I look forward to meeting you. For your information, I have also contacted Mr. Truman's widow, Amalia née Rodrigues and his brother, Dr. Martin Truman.

Best Regards,

Nicholas Wynne

CHAPTER ONE

TRYING TO BE a good father was rather like trying to sing in key, Nick thought as he watched his twelve-year-old daughter pick suspiciously at her tandoori chicken. You could be close enough that almost anyone might recognize the tune, but no one was ever going to mistake you for Frank Sinatra. And, inevitably, you managed to strike a note that simply fell flat.

"I thought you'd like Indian food," Nick said, trying not to sound reproachful. Their table was next to the window. Outside, the wet street reflected a string of red taillights and the neon sign from the cinema marquee. A waiter in black trousers and a white cotton jacket hovered nearby.

Bella set down her fork. She wore a yellow jumper that she'd coaxed Nick into buying on their last outing, and her hair was pulled back into a tight plait that came halfway down her back. "Did you ask me first?"

"Well, no, but—"

"Because if you had, I could have told you that

Mummy already tried to make me like it, and I couldn't stand it then and I still don't like it."

"Perhaps you should have said something *before* I ordered," Nick suggested. "Even as we walked into the restaurant, perhaps." Disappointment and a sense of failure made him feel churlish.

Bella seemed unaffected by his mood, her eyes—the same light green as her mother's—conveyed her disdain. Set against the olive complexion she'd inherited from him, the impact was striking. He'd look at her and envy anyone with even a modicum of artistic talent. In his head, he could wield a paintbrush in a way that captured the subtle nuance of expression, the play of light across her face. In reality, he couldn't even take a decent snapshot.

"But you enjoyed the art exhibit?" he asked. *Please tell me I'm doing something right.* Last week he'd read an article about a support group for divorced fathers. They met Monday nights in a church hall about a ten-minute walk from his North London flat. He might have made it a point to stop in, but he was leaving town—leaving the country, in fact. By the next meeting, he'd be in California, gathering material for the Truman biography that he was now under contract to write. The exhibit he'd taken his daughter to see had been a Truman retrospective.

"God forbid you'd waste a Saturday afternoon

with your daughter doing something nonproductive," Bella's mother, Avril, had remarked.

He banished his ex-wife from his thoughts. "The girl in the picture was the same age as you when—"

"Her father painted it," Bella filled in. "And her name was Daisy."

"Sorry," Nick said. "I forgot I'd already told you."

"About a hundred and fifty times."

"I've told you about two hundred and fifty times not to exaggerate," Nick said, straight-faced. "And her name *is* Daisy."

Bella looked at him.

"She's still alive and kicking," he said. "So her name *is* Daisy."

"Well, it's a very old-fashioned name," Bella said, as though that justified using the past tense. "It's like a name from a fairy story…. Or of somebody's dotty old auntie."

"Actually, she's probably just a year or two younger than me." He drank some water, and set his glass down. "Which I suppose in your books makes her an old crone."

The glimmer of a smile broke across his daughter's face. He watched her fight it. He'd angered her and, as far as she was concerned, done nothing to warrant her forgiveness. She desperately wanted to go to Laguna with him even though he and her mother, for once in agreement, had explained all the reasons why it wasn't feasible. Nick suspected that she still thought he'd ultimately relent.

Having given up any pretense of eating her chicken, she was now watching him intently as if for a clue to his final decision.

"Stop it," he said. "I know exactly what you're doing and it's not working."

Her eyes widened. "What am I doing?"

"You're trying to make me feel guilty."

"No one can *make* you feel guilty." Her voice sounded eerily like her mother's. "Only you can do that."

He regarded her with something close to wonder. How could a child almost a quarter his age sound so much like the parent? Still, she had a point. Of all the emotions he felt as a father, guilt was uppermost— he constantly berated himself for not spending enough time with her, for putting his work first, for not always being attentive when he was with her. Ironic, considering he'd been taken with Truman's portrait as much for what it suggested about the man as a father as for his skills as an artist.

For a while he'd been almost obsessed with Truman, attributing to the artist all the fatherly qualities he himself seemed to lack. And then one of the ex-wives, now dead, had written a memoir portraying Truman as a bitter, angst-ridden man who practiced the piano incessantly in case his talent as a visual artist should abandon him, who obsessively hoarded everything from toilet paper rolls and fingernail clippings to cans of food. A man who was apparently incapable of conceding he was wrong about anything.

Truman's second wife, Amalia, a one-time Portuguese fado singer, had offered a completely different perspective when Nick had reached her by phone. "Franky," as she called Truman, had all but walked on water. Amalia had appeared on the scene when Daisy was about ten; Nick had found a picture of the three of them in the archives of the weekly Laguna Beach newspaper over a wedding announcement.

The identity of Daisy's mother was still something of a mystery but one he expected to resolve once he got to the States.

"Daddy?" Bella treated him to her most soulful look. "Please?"

"Bella, I am going to Laguna to work," Nick said. "I'll be out interviewing people and, when I'm not doing that, I'll be writing. There would be nothing for you to do."

"I could watch television and go to the beach."

"And the little matter of school?"

"I'll catch up when I come back. It's only six weeks."

"We've gone over this so—"

"I hate this chicken." She glared at him. "I hate this place."

In a flash, she was up out of the booth, dragging the edge of the cloth in her haste to leave. Silverware and a water glass clattered to the floor. Nick quickly made apologies and paid the bill before going after her.

"Well, Nick, I'm sorry for stating the obvious—" his ex-wife said when he dropped a sullen and un-communicative Bella off later that night "—but it was your choice to write about an artist who lived halfway across the world. I don't suppose it occurred to you there might be subjects here in England…just a little closer to home?"

ON HIS FIRST DAY in Laguna, even before he'd unpacked his files and computer, he walked into the village and spent a great deal of money on two cotton dresses, a skirt and three shirts that the shop assistant said would be perfect for a twelve-year-old girl.

IN THE SMALL WAITING ROOM off the emergency department, Daisy Fowler tried to slow her breathing.

Amalia would be fine.

Daisy breathed deeply, sending healing thoughts to Amalia, who had just been wheeled off on a gurney, her head split open and her face the color of parchment.

Slow, deep breaths.

Amalia had called her last week, giddy with excitement. Someone was going to write Frank's life story. Daisy had also received a letter from the biographer. Same letter, very different reactions. They'd had a huge fight, and Amalia hadn't spoken to her since.

An hour ago, she'd got a call from the hospital that Amalia had fallen from her dune buggy and was in the emergency room.

There had also been a fight the night the house burned down with her father in it. "I hate you," she'd screamed.

"Lighten up, Daisy," her friend Kit was always telling her. "You're too hard on yourself. You're not responsible for other people's behaviors."

Like maybe her sixty-five-year old stepmother driving a dune buggy. Inebriated.

Deep breaths. Daisy closed her eyes and tried to meditate. She was learning the technique from a book she'd picked up last week, *How to Forgive*. The author, Baba Rama Das, pictured on the front cover, had dark, mesmerizing eyes that seemed to follow her around the room. No matter where she set the book, she'd somehow catch a glimpse of him. Yesterday, she'd felt guilty for watching *Dr. Phil* instead of meditating about forgiveness.

Forgiveness creates peace of mind, Baba said. It also helps heal emotional wounds and leads to new, more gratifying relationships. Hey, sign me up, she'd thought.

Suddenly, she felt frantic to talk to her daughter. Emmy had stomped off to catch the school bus that morning, mad over something or other. Her usual mood these days. Daisy couldn't recall the last time she and Emmy had actually talked. Really talked. A heart-to-heart kind of talk like the kind Kit regularly had with her daughter. Lately, it seemed all she and Emmy did was fight.

Still, just hearing Emmy's voice would make her feel better, more in control. She reached into her purse for the cell phone. As she punched in the number, she noticed the sign on the wall. A picture of a cell phone with a red line drawn through it. She ignored it. The answering machine came on.

"Hi sweetie," she said. "I'm at the hospital with Amalia. She had some kind of accident with the dune buggy—"

"Mom?" Emmy had picked up the phone. "What's wrong? Is she okay?"

"She's in surgery right now. She was driving up the dirt road to the highway, God knows why. I've told her enough times—"

"Just tell me."

"Well, she hit her head, which isn't good, but she's going to be okay. She *will* be okay. She'll be fine."

"Tell her I love her," Emmy said.

"I will." Daisy's nose stung with tears. "I love you too, sweetie."

Emmy had already disconnected. The cell phone rang before she had time to put it away.

"Hello, is this Daisy Fowler?"

"Yes."

"Nick Wynne. We spoke on the phone a few weeks ago...about the biography I'm writing on your father."

For a moment Daisy couldn't think of what to say. Go away came to mind. "This is a bad time," she finally managed. "I really can't talk right now." It was the same tone of voice she used on telephone solicitors. Rude and impatient, letting them know they'd intruded on her privacy. "

"I'd intended to call you in a day or so," Nick said. "But I was supposed to meet your stepmother at noon, and it's now half past one and I wondered if you might know—"

"She's in the emergency room," Daisy said. "Which is why I can't talk."

"Oh, no." A pause. "Not serious, I hope?"

"I'm waiting to find out."

"Well, look, I don't want to pester you when you obviously have other things on your mind, but I'll be here in Laguna for the next few weeks so perhaps you could give me a ring when—"

"Sure," Daisy said.

"Shall I give you my number, or—"

"Go ahead." Whatever else Nicholas Wynne said, she didn't hear. The doctor had just walked into the room.

LATER THAT NIGHT, after she'd learned that Amalia's injuries weren't serious, after she'd cooked dinner and done the dishes, helped Emmy with her homework and tried to meditate for five minutes— it was all she could manage without her thoughts going all over the place—she started feeling bad about being rude to Nicholas Wynne.

Maybe she would call tomorrow and explain that she'd just been distracted because of Amalia and, even though she wasn't that thrilled about the whole biography thing, she'd do her best to work with him.

She walked to the window and looked out at the grove of eucalyptus and beyond the trees to the clearing where she'd built the goat pen. One of the goats was trying to butt its way out, and she made a mental note to fortify the fence. The wind had picked up since the sun had gone down. Scattered about the property between tree trunks, she could see the roofs and wooden porches of the other cabins. At night, the lights from their windows twinkled like stars.

Her father had built the compound himself nearly fifty years ago, hand crafted cabins embellished with sculpture, stained glass, mosaics and wrought iron. Her father had been the consummate collector.

Her own cabin, the largest, had three bedrooms— one of which she thought of privately as her studio— and a wraparound porch. Winding gravel paths linked one structure to another. The occupants were all friends—like Kit, artists. Daisy found the sense of unity comforting. Martin, her uncle, saw it as another example of what he called her "naïve" generosity. "If they can't sell their stuff, they obviously don't have talent. They should take full-time jobs and support themselves instead of relying on you," he'd point out ad nauseam.

Building developers were always trying to get her to sell the property, but Daisy preferred to believe that her father would have liked it that she was helping a bunch of struggling artists. Collectively, they referred to themselves as the Raggle Taggle Gypsies. She'd come up with the name from an old folk song about a noble woman who ran off with the gypsies. She thought it more romantic than, say, Undisciplined Artists Who Lived Mostly Rent Free.

Unlike Daisy, none of the other cabin dwellers had inherited substantial fortunes.

"You imbecile," her father had shouted the night he died. "You stupid, stupid, girl. You utter fool," he'd thundered, pointing an imperious finger at the door. "Out of this house. I don't want to see your face again."

"Oh, I had the most perfect childhood imaginable," she pictured herself telling Nicholas Wynne. "Idyllic really. Yes, exactly. Just like the picture."

CHAPTER TWO

NICK HAD ARRANGED to meet Truman's brother Martin at the Hotel Laguna for a late breakfast. Still slightly jet-lagged, he had awakened at three, then stayed awake listening to the wind howling down the canyons. Now, five minutes early for his appointment, he strolled through the tiled lobby in the footsteps of Bette Davis, Judy Garland and Charlie Chaplin.

Laguna Beach, heart of the California Riviera, and a playground for the fabulously wealthy, a mix of artists' colony and upscale resort, of rustic beach cottages and gated mansions. The water was blue, the sand was the color of milky coffee and he couldn't look at either without thinking guiltily of Bella back in London. He would see how the work went and perhaps have her over for the last couple of weeks.

He wandered into the art-deco bar. The Grand Old Lady, as the pink stucco landmark on Pacific Coast Highway was affectionately known, had reportedly been the favorite trysting spot of Bogart and Bacall.

Truman's wife Amalia had told him that the artist had often enjoyed an evening cocktail on the balcony while he watched the sunset. He would send flowers to the hospital today, he decided.

"Nicholas."

Nick turned to see a tall and imposing man with thinning gray-black hair dressed somewhat formally for hypercasual Laguna in tan trousers and a cream sports coat. He looked like his brother, or at least the pictures Nick had seen of Truman.

After exchanging pleasantries, they moved out to the balcony and sat at one of the white wrought-iron tables. Nick craned his neck to look around. In one direction, the curve of blue and silver shoreline, in the other dark green hills tiered with terra-cotta roofs. Purple bougainvillea sprawled down the walls, red geraniums spilled from several giant urns. Realizing that Martin was watching him, he grinned self-consciously.

"Just playing awestruck tourist," he said.

"I'd like to think I never take it for granted," Martin said, "but the truth is I do. After a while, you stop seeing all this." He waved an arm to encompass the postcard-perfect scenery. "We get caught up in our lives. Have you seen much yet?"

"I just arrived two days ago, but I'd like to incorporate a bit of sightseeing." A waitress in blue jeans, tight as a second skin, and a tourniquet of yellow spandex set down water and menus, treating him to the sight of full breasts, tanned and freckled like eggs. "I'll probably wait until my daughter gets here." He drank some water. "She's incensed about having to stay in London while I'm gallivanting, as she sees it, in California."

Martin smiled. "How old is your daughter?"

"Twelve." When Martin said nothing, Nick rushed to fill the conversational void. "Child of divorced parents. Ever-present guilt." He remembered that Martin was a psychiatrist and Nick decided the silence was intended to draw him out. A tactic he often used himself. He decided not to be drawn. "And you? Children?"

"Unfortunately, no. My wife, Johanna, is a pediatric psychiatrist and we were so involved in building our practices, the time never seemed right. And then it was too late."

He took a pair of silver-rimmed glasses from the pocket of his blazer, put them on and studied the menu. Nick picked up his own menu but managed a few surreptitious glances across the table. Martin had a soft, full mouth, red-lipped and almost womanish. He'd removed the blazer, carefully draping it over the back of an empty chair. The cuffs of his off-white shirt were rolled just above the wrists, both at precisely the same length. Nick imagined him comparing them in the mirror, lining them up just so, using a tape measure perhaps. If he shared any of his late brother's artistic temperament, it wasn't evident.

The waitress arrived. Nick ordered huevos rancheros, described on the menu as fried eggs, chopped tomatoes, chili peppers, Manchego cheese and tortillas. It sounded exotic enough that he'd probably regret it later. Martin ordered half a grapefruit and a slice of whole wheat toast. Dry. They both had coffee, Martin's decaf.

Martin cleared his throat. "Regarding my brother." He aligned his knife and fork with the pale yellow linen napkin, studied the effect for a moment, then looked up, fixing his sight on a spot somewhere beyond Nick's right shoulder. "I should preface this discussion by saying that my brother had detractors. I assume you've read the…" He pursed his full lips as he appeared to seek the right word. "The piece of spiteful, slanderous garbage that his first wife threw together in an attempt to cash in on his name."

Nick nodded. This was the woman who'd written that Truman was given to raiding the bins behind supermarkets for edible discards, this after he'd amassed considerable wealth with his art.

"You're suggesting that what she wrote was untrue?"

"I'm advising you that if, as you stated in your letter, you intend to write a sympathetic, well-researched and objective biography of my brother you'll forget every word you read in that book."

"What was her motivation for writing such a book, do you suppose?"

"A woman scorned. Frank, finally seeing the light, divorced her and—since she'd already been through half his money—saw no reason to provide for her any further."

The waitress brought the food. Nick eyed his tray-sized platter. The huevos rancheros came with a small mountain of rice, bits of broken tortillas and something pale brown topped with cheese. He investigated it with his fork and glanced up at the waitress.

"Refried beans." She smiled. "Enjoy."

"You'd mentioned detractors," Nick said. "Plural."

Martin was working on his grapefruit, running a table knife around the rim of the fruit with the meticulous attention of a brain surgeon. "Amalia, his widow, while not precisely a detractor, isn't always completely truthful."

Nick looked at him.

"She has a drinking problem." He set the knife down. "Do you know about her recent accident?"

"Yes. We were supposed to meet for lunch and when she didn't arrive, I called Daisy. How is she?"

"Physically? Improving, I gather from my niece. Mentally?" He shrugged. "It all depends. She's a very flamboyant, emotional woman. Given to embroidering the truth. When Frank met her she was singing in a café in Portugal. I'd take what she says with a grain of salt."

Nick grinned. "Sorry," he said when Martin gave him a puzzled look. "Usually when I write biographies, I have access to the subject's papers. Letters, diaries, that sort of thing. In your brother's case, everything was lost in the fire. Since he was somewhat reclusive, the number of people available to me to interview is somewhat limited. His first wife's book is apparently a lie and now you're saying his widow can't entirely be trusted. It just struck me suddenly as funny. Although I should probably be gnashing my teeth."

Martin smiled faintly. "Yes, well, Daisy will be an invaluable resource. She was closer to Frank than anyone, although Amalia would have you believe that only she held the key to Frank's innermost thoughts."

"How is your relationship with Daisy?" Nick asked. "Good?"

Martin patted the napkin against his lips. "Excellent." He shrugged. "Her naïveté troubles me, but for the most part we get along."

"Frank became a father quite late in life," Nick said, moving on.

"He did. Like myself, he was focused on his profession."

"And Daisy's mother?"

"Daisy was adopted." Martin glanced around for the waitress. "More coffee would be most welcome," he muttered.

"Adopted between Frank's first and second marriages?"

Martin frowned. His thoughts seemed suddenly elsewhere. "I'm sorry," he said after a moment. "You were asking?"

"Just trying to understand the chronology. He was divorced from wife number one—"

"And then he traveled to Portugal, where he met Amalia and brought her back to Casa Athena, his home. She was here for a number of years, supported by my brother, before returning to Portugal. In the interim, my brother adopted Daisy. Just after Daisy's tenth birthday, Amalia came back to Laguna and she and Frank were married. She was with him until he died."

Nick had stopped eating as he listened to the recitation. He watched now as Martin cut a slice of toast into precise triangles, full lower lip jutting. "Were you and Frank at all alike?" he asked.

"Very much so," Martin said.

Nick tried to keep the surprise from his face. "In what ways, for example?"

"Honesty, integrity. A passion for our respective professions that precludes almost everything else."

"But Frank had a daughter," Nick said. "I know in my case, my former wife constantly complains that I put my work first. Was it difficult for Daisy, do you think? Being the daughter of a respected and prolific artist?"

Martin, having eaten his toast and grapefruit, folded his napkin and placed it on his plate. "I know nothing of your personal situation, of course, but Frank had a unique ability. I'd said his passion for art precluded *almost* everything else. The *almost* being Daisy. My brother had the unique ability to…how shall I put it, integrate the love he had for his daughter into his art."

Nick thought of seeing Truman's artwork for the first time. The rainy, London street outside, the sunlit cliff and the smiling girl on the canvas inside. "Yes. I saw that in his work," he said truthfully. "Which is why I'm writing this biography."

"TODAY'S LESSON in self-improvement, in case you're interested, is about not feeling resentful and put-upon," Daisy told Kit. "But Toby's doing his usual shtick, Amalia's calling every five minutes from the hospital, Emmy's being impossible and I'm supposed to drop everything and sit patiently while some guy I don't know from Adam asks me to reminisce about my father."

"You sound resentful and put-upon," Kit said.

"I guess I need to work a little harder, huh?"

They were drinking guava-flavored iced tea and

watching for the school bus as it lumbered its way up Laguna Canyon Road to drop off their daughters. Daisy was wearing a shirt that read, I Live In My Own World, But It's Okay, They Know Me Here. She and Kit were both wearing flip-flops. Daisy's were a pink-and-white candy-striped rubber version with a pink daisy on the toepiece; Kit's were lime-green translucent plastic. They'd picked up four pairs—a pair each for them and for the girls—the day before at the end-of-season sale at the Village Drug Store.

Daisy looked at their feet side by side on the wooden deck rail. Kit's were a dark olive color, her toenails painted deep burgundy, which, in the dappled shade, looked almost black. Her own feet were freckled, her toes unpainted, although Emmy was always offering to paint them, or encouraging her to get a pedicure. Emmy, to her perpetual disgust, had inherited Daisy's tendency to burn rather than turn lusciously caramel like every other kid in Laguna, or golden-brown like her father.

"So how is Amalia?" Kit asked.

"Doing okay, I guess." A broken wrist and a cracked rib, but her alcohol level had been above the legal limit and a social worker had suggested counseling, which Amalia would never do in a million years because, of course, she doesn't think she has a problem. "I'm trying to talk her into coming here for a few days. If she goes back to that cottage, she's going to drag out all those old pictures of my dad, drink, get maudlin and…"

Kit looked at her. "She's not suicidal or anything?"

"No, but when she drinks she starts thinking about my dad and… I mean, really, that's one of the things that really irritates me about this whole biography thing. Not that I don't have my own reservations, but Amalia knows damn well she can't mention Dad's name without getting teary eyed. But she and Martin voted me down when I said we should tell the guy no. Martin starts doing his psychiatrist shtick and telling me I need to confront my fears or some garbage and Amalia tells me I'm selfish. Even Toby gets in on the act and Emmy—"

"Hey." Kit leaned over to wrap her arm around Daisy's shoulder. "Deep, deep breaths. Everything happens for a reason. Remember that. Listen, I'm going to walk up to the road to meet the girls. Want to walk with me?"

Daisy shook her head. "I'm just going to stay here and veg…I mean breathe…. *Meditate* is what I'm trying to say."

She watched as Kit made her way through the grove of eucalyptus and down the dirt road that led to the highway. It was warm for early November, even by Southern California standards, and the dogs were sprawled in whatever patch of shade they could find: under the thick growth of the pepper tree, beneath the steps of the cabin. Little brown Allie, Daisy's favorite, was curled up beneath the Adirondack chair. The goats, five of them, had retreated to their shed, and the three cats were off somewhere doing their own inscrutable cat thing.

The wind was picking up. The Santa Anas, hot dry winds that blew in from the desert and made everyone feel cranky. They'd been linked to industrial accidents, lower test scores, kids misbehaving in school, heart attacks, all that sort of thing. They also whipped up wildfires like the one burning a few miles to the north.

The Santa Anas had been blowing the day her father had died in the fire that destroyed Casa Athena and everything in it.

The boom box on the deck was tuned to a country-western station. "*I can feel it in the wind*," some guy was singing. "*There's trouble blowin' in*." Weird, it had been playing on the truck stereo when she had driven home from the hospital last night. **Signs are all around**, she'd read in the *Forgiveness* book. You just have to be observant.

The winds freaked her though. She'd lived in California her entire life, and they were as much a part of the state as the ocean surf, but it was the same every year. As a child, she'd lain awake listening to them beat against the roof. Things would pry loose and blow away in this terrifying orchestra of sound that would send her shaking and sobbing into the safety of her father's room where she'd burrow quivering beneath the blankets. The next morning, the sky was as innocent and blue as a child's eyes, but the torn tree limbs and hurled garden furniture were witnesses to the nocturnal rampage.

The phone rang. She decided to let the machine pick it up.

From where she sat, she could hear the English accent. Nicholas Wynne.

"I hope your stepmother's on the mend and, of course, I still very much want to talk to you. It's quite incredible being here in Laguna, actually seeing the places your father painted. Please give me a call at your earliest convenience."

A fly buzzed annoyingly around her face and she swatted it with her hand, then she got up, took the iced tea pitcher inside and stuck it in the sink. In the fridge, she found a carton of leftover Chinese takeout. She carried it into the living room and flipped on the TV.

Dr. Phil was talking about emotional eating, of all things. Of using food as comfort. Daisy feigned surprise. *People do that?* She watched as he reduced a fat woman in a red dress to tears, then decided watching other people's pain when there was nothing you could do to help them was a sick kind of voyeurism. Kind of like being a biographer, when she stopped to think about it. Maybe she'd suggest a quid pro quo. "I'll tell you about my life, if you tell me about yours." But then what did she care about Nicholas Wynne or his life?

CHAPTER THREE

"WITH RISING TEMPERATURES and Santa Ana winds stoking fires throughout Southern California, the question on the minds of many in Laguna Beach is, Can it happen again?"

Nick slumped on the sofa, and gazed bleary-eyed at the TV. Late morning sunshine poured in through the French doors, heating the room to tropical temperatures. He sneezed, then sneezed again. He wore the white terry-cloth robe that had been in the bathroom, along with other niceties, such as shoe-cleaning cloths and lavender-scented body wash—compensation, he supposed, for the small fortune he was paying for an oceanfront apartment. A justifiable expense since this would be his definitive work. The work that would earn him a vast quantity of money, enough to take Bella on holidays to exotic destinations, indulge her every whim and, possibly, buy himself the silver Porsche Carrera GT he'd salivated over in the showroom window of Laguna Motors yesterday.

I should get up and open the doors, he thought. *I should turn off the TV and start work. I should try to reach Daisy Fowler again.* He was starting to feel mildly rejected by Daisy Fowler and just a bit disappointed in her.

He sneezed again. And again.

He'd awakened just before dawn, sneezing his head off. Allergies, apparently from the winds that blew like demons and kept him awake half the night. At one point, he'd been certain someone was breaking into his apartment. Grabbing a shoe, the only thing remotely weaponlike he could find, he'd crept into the living room. The noise, he'd discovered, was a plastic plate, probably blown from somebody's rubbish bin, hitting the glass of the French windows.

On TV, a reporter was interviewing a fire chief.

The current weather, Nick learned, was eerily similar to conditions fourteen years ago when flames ravaged the local scenic canyons and hills, destroying hundreds of homes in and around Laguna Beach.

"It's not a question of *if* fire will revisit Laguna Beach," the fire chief was saying. "It's a question of *when.*"

He would have to remember to tell Bella. *"It's a good thing you didn't come, darling. No really. Fires burning everywhere. Entire hillsides blazing. No, no, the beaches haven't burned up, but still..."*

He sneezed. He got up from the couch, sat down at the table where he'd put up his computer. He thought about Daisy. Perhaps he'd built up an image of her that no actual woman could live up to. The golden-haired child basking in the sunlight of her father's love, grown into an ethereal goddess…who had an ex-husband, a fourteen-year-old daughter and goats. And who didn't return his phone calls. He mulled this for a while, tried to come up with plausible reasons why she might *not* want to talk to him. He sneezed. Difficult to think while sneezing. He returned to the couch.

He had lined up some other interviews over the next few days. A woman from the Laguna Historical Society who knew Frank from years ago; another breakfast, this one with a gallery owner who had worked with Truman. All peripheral to the biography, though. Truman's relationship with Daisy as reflected in his art was the central theme of the work. Truman was dead, so no one else really mattered but Daisy. He would give her until this evening and if she hadn't called, he'd leave another message. Sending more flowers might be overdoing it. He thought about driving past her house. He sneezed.

He was considering spending the entire day on the couch watching the telly when the phone rang.

Valerie, his girlfriend in England. She had also wanted to come with him to Laguna, but things with

Valerie were rocky. Actually the entire six-month relationship had never been anything but rocky, rooted mostly in sex and a mutual fondness for tandoori takeout. He listened as she complained at length about the dreary weather in London and her life of late, also dreary.

"It's horrible, Nick. I'm honestly not sure how much more I can take."

"Maybe it would help if you got away for a bit," Nick said. Actually, driving by Daisy Fowler's house might not be a bad idea. He could be casually passing by just as she happened to walk out. Although her uncle had said something about her living in a compound off a dirt road, which might make casually passing by difficult to explain.

"D'you think so?" Valerie's voice had brightened. "Maybe you're right."

"Absolutely."

"Brilliant. Well, I'll get started on it right away. How are things with you?"

Nick sneezed.

"Is that a good thing?"

"Allergies," Nick said. "Wind's stirring up dust and pollen and God knows what. It's having a rather debilitating effect on me."

"Maybe I shouldn't read the review of your Bongiovanni book, then," Valerie said, a note of hesitation in her voice. "It ran in this morning's *Times*."

Nick stared, unseeing now, at the TV. He steeled himself. "Favorable?"

"Shall I read it?"

"Broad strokes will do."

"You'll get angry…"

"I won't get angry, damn it. Do you have the review there?"

"I'm looking at it right now. It's not *bad* exactly."

"For God's sake—"

"It just says that you…it, the biography, doesn't add anything to what we already know about Bongiovanni. That was a quote. It also said you held him, Bongiovanni, at arm's length, that you never really got to the heart of who he was. Inconclusive, that's another quote and, hold on, here it is. Shallow and superfici—"

"Right."

"More?"

"No."

He carried the phone into the kitchen, took a carton of orange juice from the fridge and set it on the counter. He'd had his hopes set on *definitive*. *Wynne has written the definitive biography of Bongiovanni. In this uncompromisingly honest work, Wynne has captured the soul of the tenor.* He decided he didn't want orange juice after all. He went back into the living room and collapsed on the couch.

"Nick?"

"What?"

"You're not sulking, are you?"

"Don't be so stupid," he said sulkily. "Sulking about what?"

"The review."

"Already forgotten about it." Already mentally composing the vituperative letter he would write to the *Times* railing about the sheer idiocy of the reviewer who…or maybe biting sarcasm would be more the ticket. He'd think about it later.

"How's the current project?" she asked.

"The daughter could prove to be something of a roadblock. I sense resistance."

"The daughter?"

"Daisy. The child in the pictures, except she's now about forty, has a daughter and runs a restaurant here in Laguna with her ex-husband."

"Why is she resisting?"

"Well, I'd have to ask her, wouldn't I? Which I would if she'd answer her bloody phone. I've lost count of the messages I've left. Ignored every one of them. Apparently she lives in a wooden cabin on the outskirts of town and keeps goats."

"Goats?"

"Hires them out to homeowners who live in the hills." He'd learned this from Martin, who had called earlier to check on his progress. "The goats eat the brush, which works to keep the fire danger down. That's how Truman died. Burned to death in his home."

"How ghastly. Maybe that's why the daughter doesn't want to talk. Maybe it's all too painful for her."

Nick considered. "It's been fourteen years."

"It *was* her father, Nick," Valerie said reprovingly.

He sneezed again and blew his nose. He felt like hell.

"Would it be better if I booked to San Diego?" Valerie was asking.

"Sorry?"

"When I come over. Would it be better if I book into L.A. or San Diego?"

"I thought you were talking about going to your sister's in Kent."

"Which sister?"

"How many sisters do you have?"

"Two. Neither of them lives in Kent." She sighed. "Do you ever listen to anything I say?"

"I heard you say you needed to get away."

"*You* said I needed to get away. That was *your* suggestion."

"*My* suggestion?"

"Nick, have you been drinking? You sound… odd."

"I'm unwell." The television was showing pictures of orange flame rolling like molten lava down a hillside. The sight momentarily distracted him. "You should see this," he told Valerie. "Houses burning all over the place, sheets of flame shooting up into the sky. It's incredible. They're showing someone leading horses down a hillside, and the fires look as though they're just a few feet away."

"That happens in California, doesn't it?" Valerie asked. "It seems there's always one disaster or another. The price of living in paradise, I suppose." She paused. "Still, at least it's warm. And it's not raining, is it? There's a lot to be said for nice weather. What are the beaches like?"

"Covered in ash."

"Oh, come on. It can't be that bad."

"Look Val," he said. "I told Bella she couldn't come because I needed to work, and I'm telling you the same thing. I'm trying not to be superstitious, but I get here on the day Truman's widow lands in hospital, so obviously I can't talk to her for a while. Then the daughter, who's central to the whole book, is proving difficult….." He sneezed. "Excuse me. Let's talk about something else, all right?"

But there wasn't much else that Valerie wanted to talk about, and after they'd said their goodbyes Nick picked up the phone and punched in Daisy's number again.

"My mom?" a young girl asked. "Sorry, she's not here."

Of course she isn't. "I've left several messages," he said. "She must be very busy."

"Yeah, she is, kind of."

"You must be…"

"Emily. Except everyone calls me Emmy."

"And you've attained the ripe old age of fourteen."

A beat of silence. "How d'you know that?"

"I'm omniscient," he said. "It just came to me in a flash of lavender-colored smoke."

"Seriously."

"I'm a biographer. I snoop for a living."

She laughed. "I'll tell my mom you called."

"Thank you, Emily. I enjoyed our little chat."

"Me, too," she said. "Bye."

Nick was smiling as he hung up. He called Bella but got her mother.

"She's next door at her friend's," Avril said.

"Isn't it past her bedtime?"

"Not for a couple of hours. Anything else about your daughter I can fill you in on?"

Ran out of mood stabilizers, did you? "Just tell her I called, please. I'll try again tomorrow, or she can call me here."

"Actually, while I have you on the phone, Bella's in love with this little cottage in Devon. We took the train down there last week just to get away from the city for a bit and—well, her disappointment about you know what—and lo and behold, there it was. A sweet cottage that we could use on weekends and school holidays…I did put in an offer, but now I'm having second thoughts. I haven't broken the news to Bella yet, she'll be devastated."

Nick's left eye had started to itch uncontrollably. He sneezed. Now his right eye was tearing. "Why are you having second thoughts?"

"It's rather a stretch financially, I'm not sure—"

"Go ahead," he said impulsively. "I'll make up whatever you need."

"Nick. My God, are you absolutely sure?"

"I got a decent advance for the Truman book," he said.

"Bella will be over the moon. She was terribly disappointed about the Laguna thing—"

"Yes, I know," he said. "Well, I hope this helps."

THE VAGUE SENSE OF DOOM he'd felt after making the offer stayed with him for the rest of the morning. Daisy Fowler had no idea of course, but she had the power to make his life very, very difficult.

Later that night, he wandered down to the Hotel Laguna and had a couple of beers on the balcony while he watched the sun set over the Pacific. Instead of uplifting him, though, he found himself sinking into a morose gloom. The words of the Bongiovanni review lingered like an ill-digested meal *"Arm's length,"* indeed. He sipped his beer. Gloom gave way to anger. He'd show them arm's length. He was going to write the definitive biography of Frank Truman, and he would take no prisoners in the process. Darling Daughter Daisy be damned.

"YOUR GRANDFATHER, he was a very handsome man," Amalia was telling Emily. "All the girls, they fell in love with him because he was so funny and so big and strong."

"Dinner's almost ready, you guys," Daisy called from the kitchen of Amalia's cottage. "Emmy, get those pictures cleared off the table so we can sit down." She and Emmy had brought Amalia home from the hospital that morning. Predictably, Amalia had insisted on coming back to the place where she said Frank still lived in the walls and the shadows, and where the ocean that crashed onto the beach brought gifts of pale pink seashells that were also from Frank.

Daisy sighed. How could you argue with that? All you could do was case the cabin for booze bottles and accidentally on purpose hide the keys to the dune buggy so she wouldn't take it into town until she'd recovered completely.

She set the enchilada casserole under the broiler in Amalia's yellowing enameled stove, washed up the dishes she'd used in the deep, square sink, chipped and stained from years of use. On the draining board was a jelly jar of purple statice Emmy had picked to welcome Amalia home from the hospital.

As she took the plates from the cupboard, she spotted the fifth of vodka. She set the plates down, uncapped the bottle, poured it down the sink and stuffed it to the bottom of the trash can.

"It is very sad that you never knew your grandfather," Amalia was telling Emily. "But a good thing that this man, Mr. Wynne, is writing a book about him because you will learn many things about him that maybe you didn't know."

Which is part of the problem, Daisy thought. There had been another message from Nicholas Wynne that morning. She checked the casserole— not ready yet. Amalia's antiquated stove took forever to heat up.

She opened the back door to the balcony. A cool breeze off the ocean tossed her hair. Fog had obscured the moon. The surrounding cottages, empty in the winter months, were dark. Amalia's cottage was at the end of a cluster of twenty that lined Dolphin Cove's crescent-shaped beach. Before she was born, her father had used the cottage as his studio, and he and Amalia had spent summers there—fairly wild summers, she'd gathered from bits and pieces dropped by Amalia over the years. Above the fireplace was a painting of Amalia in a 1950s-era bathing suit, draped against a fin-tailed Cadillac convertible bristling with old wooden surfboards.

Pictures—of Amalia, of Amalia with Frank, of Amalia and Frank with other handsome, windblown, sun-kissed friends—lined every square inch of wall space. All were taken in the first half of her father's relationship with her stepmother. Before Daisy, or B.D., as she often thought of it. Something had happened right before she was born, and Amalia had left.

The second phase of the Frank and Amalia relationship began on the day of her tenth birthday. She'd come down to breakfast, excited about the presents she knew would be waiting for her and found only this exotic-looking woman with huge gold rings in her ears and a red chiffon scarf tied around her head. "Say good morning to Amalia," her father had said. "She's made flan for breakfast."

"It's my birthday," she'd blurted. "Where are my presents?"

Frank had pointed to Amalia. "Happy birthday. Meet your new mother."

And that was it. No explanation. No little talk beforehand. "Honey, a very dear friend has come back into my life. I hope you will learn to love her as much as I do…but if for any reason you'd rather she left, just say the word. You're always first in my life."

Hah. Amalia had taken over the kitchen, always making dishes with too much spice and big chunks of unidentifiable meat. She'd play this weird, sad music that nothing drowned out, and she and Frank were always kissing and giggling and tickling each other.

"Either she goes or I do," she'd told her father about six weeks after Amalia appeared at the kitchen table. "I was here before she was and it's not fair."

"Amalia was here long before you were," he'd responded. "And life's not fair."

"Where's my real mother?" she'd screamed. "I'm going to live with her."

"Write me," her father had said.

Years later, long after she'd accepted Amalia as a stepmother, she'd asked again about her real mother. Amalia claimed not to know. "I came back to your father and found him with a daughter. Frank never wanted me to ask questions."

"Your real mother?" her father had smiled. "Who would you like her to be? Mother Teresa? Dolly Parton? Mae West?"

"Hey, Mom." Emmy appeared on the balcony. "What's burning?"

"Damn." She darted inside and opened the oven. "Caught it in the nick of time."

"Nick," Emily said, following her.

Daisy looked up from the casserole.

"That just reminded me. Nick called."

"The biographer?" Daisy raised an eyebrow. "Since when has he been Nick?"

Emmy rolled her eyes. "Jeez, Mom. That's what he said his name was. He sounds nice. Kind of like… Hugh Grant. You know, in *Bridget Jones's Diary*."

Daisy nodded. They'd rented the video last week. "But Hugh Grant wasn't really nice, was he? He was deceitful and—"

"Jeez, Mom. Chill out," Emmy said.

Daisy carried the casserole to the table, where she had to shove aside a gigantic vase of yellow roses to make room for it. As she did, a card fell out.

To Amalia. I hope that doesn't strike an overly familiar note, but on some level I feel as if I know you already. In any event, I wish you a speedy recovery and am looking forward to meeting you in person and learning all about your late husband. Warmly, Nicholas Wynne.

"Emily!" Daisy yelled to her daughter, who had wandered outside. "Are you going to help me, or do I have to do everything around here?"

CHAPTER FOUR

THAT NIGHT DAISY couldn't sleep. In his book Baba talked about forgiving and how, when you did, the heart opened like a bud. But sometimes, even now, when she thought about her father she could feel her own heart snap shut. Or maybe it was more like the lid of a trunk slamming down on all the things you never wanted to think about again. All the things, good and bad, jumbled in there together. What was she supposed to do? Just hand them all to this biographer and say, "Here, you sort it all out"?

Lately, there were days when she saw her father's face in everything. This morning it had been the pair of black rubber Wellington boots, hers, aligned neatly on the cabin's back porch next to a pot of red geraniums.

She'd just finished feeding the goats and had started up the path to the cabin when she happened to glance down at the front step. And there was her father with his sun-faded blue eyes and year-round tan and the gleeful expression of a child as he rambled on about something he'd done that he wasn't going to tell her about because he wanted it to be a surprise. And he was wearing a big, clomping, olive-green version of the boots he'd bought her in Paris at a shop near the Pompidou Center, where they'd also sold chickens and rabbits in cages. He'd made her put on her boots and they'd gone tromping down to the fields to check out his surprise, which had been an old wrought-iron birdcage that he'd hung from the bare branches of an almond tree. Inside, he'd perched a yellow plastic bird of indeterminate species. It was the incongruity that had delighted him.

A good memory. And then there was the one about rain.

She'd been in the bathroom getting dressed for school and she'd called out to ask if it was raining. He'd said it wasn't, but when she'd looked outside it was pouring down. He'd flown into a rage when she questioned him. His definition of rain was obviously different from hers, he'd yelled. This was just a heavy mist, nothing more than a drizzle, and why did she even ask if she didn't want his opinion?

Maybe it would have been funny if he hadn't been so furious.

Would that be a memory to share with Nicholas Wynne?

She glanced at the bedside clock. Two-thirty. God, she was going to be a basket case tomorrow. She got up, pulled on a sweatshirt and padded barefoot to the kitchen. The refrigerator, a more reliable source of emotional solace than Baba—she felt guilty thinking that, but it was true—yielded only cheese, milk, peanut butter and some yellowing broccoli. But then, hidden away behind a tub of nonfat yogurt, she spotted a bag of chocolate chips.

She would hate herself for this when she got on the scales tomorrow, she thought as she finally drifted off to sleep.

The next time she opened her eyes, it was nine-fifteen.

Damn. She jumped out of bed and headed for the kitchen. And found Toby, her ex-husband, sitting there with Emily, both of them laughing.

Emmy laughing. Daisy shook her head. It was a sound she hadn't heard in weeks. They were so deep in whatever was making them laugh that neither of them saw her in the doorway. There was a box of Cocoa Krispies on the table, two blue bowls and a gallon of milk. Emmy finally glanced up, saw Daisy and her smile faded to a scowl.

"Our little girl wants to go to culinary school," Toby said. "What do you think about that, Daze?"

Daisy grunted something noncommittal. She and Toby ran a restaurant together, Wildfire. He was the chef, she made desserts. When they opened it last year and she'd let it slip to Martin that she'd financed it, he'd told her she needed to have her head examined. "Just don't come complaining to me when Toby acts up, as he will," he'd warned. "The restaurant business is notoriously fickle, and going into partnership with your ex-husband, much less a character like Toby, is just asking for trouble."

"I was telling Emmy, it's about time she started dressing up to show off how good-looking she's getting," Toby was saying.

And I've been telling her just the opposite, Daisy thought. She noticed that Emmy, who flew into a rage at even the mildest criticism of what she was wearing, was carefully avoiding her eye.

Toby, after a few more unsuccessful attempts to engage her in conversation, announced that he'd better get going. He left—cereal bowl filmed with milk and glued-on bits of Cocoa Krispies still on the table. Emmy had retreated to her room.

Daisy carried the bowl to the sink, put the cereal away and wiped off the table. An image came to her of her father at the stove. He'd never slept well, often getting up around dawn to make breakfast, an activity that involved hollering and playing marching music and singing at the top of his voice— just in case she might still be sleeping. None of it had bothered Amalia, who could sleep through anything.

On that particular morning she remembered, he'd

been wearing a chef's hat, brandishing a wooden spoon like a conductor's baton as he'd belted out tunes.

She'd got her camera and snapped off half a dozen shots before he realized what she was doing. After the film was developed, he'd critiqued the pictures. "Not bad, not bad. But notice how the spoon is slightly out of focus and you've got all this clutter in the background and, this is just constructive criticism, honey, but see the way the clock on the wall seems to be coming out of my head...."

It had been the same with every picture she'd taken. She'd examine them for hours before she submitted them to him, convinced she'd finally mastered perfection. She'd never even come close. After a while she'd lost interest in photography all together.

Another memory to share with Nicholas Wynne?

The phone rang. She took a deep breath and picked up the receiver.

Nicholas Wynne.

"My God, I was beginning to think you were a figment of my imagination," he said. "Either that, or you were avoiding me."

Daisy sat at the kitchen table. This guy sounded a tad too chipper for the mood she was in. "A lot of stuff going on," she said.

"How *is* your stepmother, by the way?"

Sober, I hope. And taking her asthma medicine. And staying off the dune buggy. "Improving," she said.

"I've left a couple of messages, but haven't heard back," he said.

"You're kind of batting zero all around."

"Sorry?" He paused then laughed. "Oh, right. I've left one or two with you, too, haven't I? Anyway, I wondered if we could meet for lunch in the next day or so. I thought perhaps the Ritz Carlton. A favorite of your father's, I understand."

"So was Tio Taco's," Daisy said.

"Would you like to meet there, then?"

"It burned down ten years ago."

"Right… That's out then. Back to the Ritz?"

"The Ritz isn't my kind of place," Daisy said. "The Ritz stuff was before my time…before I was born, I mean."

"Do you have a suggestion?"

Go back to England. "Why my father?" she asked.

"Why do I want to write about him specifically?"

"Yeah."

"Well, as I explained in my letter, I was intrigued by something in his painting. I'm not much of an art enthusiast, I'm the sort who buys a picture because it goes with the couch. But I'd seen your father's painting and I felt more hopeful somehow."

"Kind of a lot to take away from a painting," Daisy said.

"You've never felt that way? Moved in a way you can't explain by a piece of art or music …"

Daisy shrugged although obviously he couldn't see her. Chopin did that to her, but she wasn't about to say so. "That was it? You saw the painting and decided to write a book about him?"

"Well, I did some research, of course."

"How?"

"Newspaper articles, other published works about him."

"His first wife's book?"

"Uh…I'm taking all that with a grain of salt," he said.

Martin had probably told him to take it with a whole saltshaker full. Except a lot of it was actually true. "So, how is a biography different from gossip?" She could hear a tone in her voice that sounded exactly like her father. Not just questioning but truculent, spoiling for a fight. She couldn't stop herself. "I mean, you read this juicy stuff about him written by an enemy, say. How do you even know it's true? Who even decides it's true?" Her voice went up a notch. "Maybe she's lying through her teeth."

"That's entirely possible," Nicholas said. "Which is why I talk to as many people as I can."

"Even so. Memories are so…circumstantial. Say I was in a bad mood, maybe some little thing I told you would make him sound dark and gloomy, or not a very nice person. But say I'd just made this incredible pot of salsa, and the smell of it was like a bouquet of flowers and the sun was shining through the door. I could tell you the same story and it would come out completely different."

"I'll just have to catch you on a day when the cooking's going well," he said.

Daisy gave up. Baba talked about creating false obstacles—reacting to your thoughts instead of to real situations. Maybe this guy would just ask a bunch of puffball questions. She'd give him warm, fuzzy answers and that would be that.

"I own a restaurant in town with my ex-husband," she said. "Wildfire. I'll be there tomorrow around five if you want to drop by."

As soon as she hung up, she wanted to call back to say she'd changed her mind. What if he wanted real information? Could you simultaneously yearn for the truth but be so terrified of looking too closely that you were always averting your eyes?

The phone rang again. It was Amalia.

"Your father came to me in my dream last night, Daisy." She sounded shrill, almost hysterical. "He is very, very angry about the book."

"The book? You mean the biography?"

"He said no. No book."

Daisy walked outside and sat down on the porch steps. The dogs stopped chasing squirrels to join her.

Amalia was always having dreams about Frank telling her what to do. "Did he say why?"

"Frank does not explain himself," Amalia said. "When he says no book, he means no book. He has always been that way. He says terrible things will happen if it is written."

Daisy imagined tomorrow's conversation with Nick. "Sorry to disappoint you, but my father said no book."

"He was very, very angry," Amalia said. "He doesn't want this stranger to write about him."

"Amalia…" Daisy sighed. "Look, the guy has come all the way from England. I mean, I've never been that jazzed about the biography, but you and Martin both wanted it. I can't tell him it's off just because you had a dream."

"This dream was very, very real. I saw Frank as if he was standing in front of my eyes. He said bad things will happen."

"What kind of bad things?"

"You don't want to know," Amalia said. "But very, very bad. I was wrong. Daisy, please, you have to tell this Nicholas no."

"Okay." She hung up the phone. It rang almost immediately. Amalia again. Even over the phone she could hear her stepmother wheezing.

"Okay, okay. Use your inhaler. I'm going to meet

him tomorrow. I'll tell him. Listen, I've got to go. I'll call you later."

As she grabbed her keys and started for the door, the phone rang again. Guessing it was Amalia, she grabbed it.

"This is American Express," a woman said. "We're calling to make sure you actually made a purchase that's about to be charged to your account. It's a little out of the ordinary for your spending habits and…"

"What's the purchase?"

"A salamander."

"A what?"

"Thirty-five hundred dollars. From the Culinary King."

Daisy scratched her head. A salamander was some kind of reptile, right? Then enlightenment dawned. Toby had apparently ordered another expensive toy that Wildfire couldn't do without. "No," she said. "Don't approve it. I need to talk to the buyer first."

As she sprinted to the truck, she glanced up at the sky. "Okay, what gives? Have I offended someone up there, or something?"

CHAPTER FIVE

NICK WAS SO RELIEVED at not only making contact with Daisy, finally, but actually setting up a time to meet her that he couldn't focus on anything that required sitting quietly at the computer. Laguna was still waiting to be explored, and it seemed a perfect time to find out more about the world Frank Truman had once inhabited.

He left the apartment, strolled around the tree-lined streets for half an hour or so, people-watched the bronzed and beautiful from the vantage point of a sidewalk café and walked some more. On a side street off Pacific Coast Highway, he came to the restaurant Daisy had mentioned. He walked into the courtyard filled with a jungle of greenery. The front door was locked, but he could see through into the sleek glass and chrome dining room and part of the kitchen beyond where a chef was working.

The chef saw him and waved. In one of those bits of serendipity that occasionally brighten the day, the chef, it turned out, was none other than Toby Fowler, and he was only too glad to help in any way he could.

Thirty minutes later, Nick had drawn at least one conclusion about Daisy's ex-husband. After listening to him hold forth on everything from the most flavorful wood to use for smoking meat (apple) to where in Laguna to meet "the hottest chicks," (Main Beach), Nick had decided that, for all the talk about other women, Toby was still struggling with unresolved feelings for his ex-wife.

One clue was his apparent inability to stop talking about her. No matter the topic, everything eventually led back to Daisy. He watched Toby sharpen a lethal-looking knife—Daisy hadn't wanted him to buy it, of course, which was further proof, according to Toby, that she knew nothing about running a restaurant. As Toby talked, Nick tried hard to reconcile Daisy, the golden child in the paintings, with Daisy the ex-wife of this stocky, muscled man with the bleached blond crew cut. Somehow he couldn't quite manage it.

Toby was rattling on about how Daisy never did this and was always doing that. Why, Nick wondered, were solutions to the romantic agonies of others (get over her, for God's sake, she's clearly not worth it) so much more obvious than one's own? Perhaps he should consult Toby on whether or not to encourage Valerie's visit.

"The thing with Daisy is, if she believes something's good or bad or whatever," Toby said, "no way can she accept there might be another way of looking at things."

"How exactly do you mean?" Nick asked.

"Like her father, for instance." He stopped. "Look you didn't hear this from me, okay? I don't want Daisy coming down on me for dissing her father, but everyone knows he was nutty as a fruit cake. Would Daisy admit that though? Uh-uh. He was *eccentric*. Different. Emotional. Nuts? Not a chance."

Nick was interested. "Did you know him?"

"I stayed out of his path as much as I could. Didn't *want* to be around him. Daisy put up with stuff from him that no one in their right mind would take. I was the one who had to calm her down after he'd yelled and screamed at her for something or other. He was this famous artist though, so it was okay for him to yell and scream. Anyone else would have the police knocking on the door."

Nick wondered if Martin considered Toby one of Frank Truman's detractors. Maybe the truth lay somewhere between Martin Truman's version and that of the mendacious first wife.

Toby brought the blade down with a hard *thwack*. "You know what else drives me nuts about her? That bunch of freeloading hippy friends she's got living up on her property." He disappeared behind the door of a massive stainless-steel refrigerator, emerged with a tray of steaks. "Well, she calls them friends. Problem is, they're all on the take. You ever been up to her place?"

Nick said he hadn't.

"She lives in this cabin on about three acres of land off Laguna Canyon Road. It's worth millions, but Daisy doesn't care. Her father built the cabins back in the fifties for these big-time artist friends from Los Angeles who came down to Laguna on weekends. Not a load of deadbeats like Daisy's got living there."

"Do they pay rent?"

"'Oh Daisy,'" he said in a mincing voice, "'my kitty cat got sick and I had to take her to the vet and now I don't have enough money to pay the rent.'" In another falsetto, this presumably Daisy's, Toby said, "'Just pay me when you have the money.' Right."

"Maybe she thinks of it as carrying on her father's legacy," Nick said. "Helping struggling artists, that sort of thing."

Toby made a dismissive gesture. "If what they do is art, then I'm Chef Boyardee. They call themselves artists, but none of them has ever sold a damn thing."

Nick imagined himself approaching Daisy, who apparently had a blind spot for a sob story. Tin cup in his outstretched hand. *Please Miss Daisy, talk to me. This biography will put food on my table. I haven't eaten for months.*

"The thing you gotta know about Daisy is she has a heart as big as all outdoors. She kind of went to pieces after her father died. Gained a ton of weight.

She's dropped it, but she doesn't look the way she did when I first knew her. It's like she's, I don't know, gone into herself."

"So she doesn't talk about her father to you?"

Toby shook his head. "Doesn't talk about him to anyone. After he died, she just stopped talking about him, period."

"How long have you known her?" Nick asked.

Toby shrugged. "We grew up together, like, but I didn't really get to know her until about a year before the old man died. She was kind of lonely then, no one else to turn to."

He'd started cutting the meat into wafer-thin slices, every move careful and exact. A muscle twitched in his cheek, his jaw was tense. Anger offered another clue that Toby still had a thing for his ex-wife. People got incensed at those they didn't love, of course, but there was a certain quality to the kind of anger that was all mixed up with having once loved the person who has caused your wrath, making it burn with a particular intensity. Toby was clearly smoldering.

"Naturally, she forgets all that now. She's got all her hippy friends who are happy to listen to her. Hell, it's cheaper than paying rent, right?" He shook his head. "To be honest with you, Daisy drives me nuts, but…I dunno, sometimes I think it's too bad we can't just make things work again. I mean, we have a kid and everything…but Daisy's so damn stubborn."

And you're in love with her, Nick thought. Was it mutual? Maybe just a sticky patch on the matrimonial road? His own experience had proved, ultimately, to be less sticky patch than insurmountable block. He realized that he felt sorry for Toby. If he could have come up with some words of wisdom, he would have.

"You haven't met Daisy yet, right?" Toby asked.

"Tomorrow."

Toby rolled his eyes. "Good luck. She's not the easiest person to be around these days."

WHY HAD SHE AGREED to meet the guy? *Why?* It was four o'clock and Daisy was in the kitchen on the phone with a hysterical Amalia, mindlessly devouring a bowl of Wacky-cake batter. She put the bowl in the fridge, leaned against the door and breathed slowly.

"Amalia, listen to me, okay? Just listen." She moved to the table and sat down. "I don't understand why you're getting so worked up over this dream—"

"I tell you, Daisy, it was so real. You should have been there to see your father's face. Please promise me you will tell Mr. Wynne there is no book."

"I'm meeting him in an hour." She scratched a spot of hardened candlewax from the tabletop. "Look, don't get mad, okay? This whole dream thing? You just seem to be, I don't know, overreacting a little. Are you sure something else isn't bothering you?"

Amalia started crying. "You didn't hear Franky's voice. You didn't see his face. Oh, Daisy, please—"

"Okay, okay." God, next she'd be driving Amalia to the emergency room. "Look, it's okay. I'll tell him it's off. I promise. Just calm down. And use your inhaler. I'll call you later."

She put the phone down. From Emily's bedroom, she could hear the *thump, thump, thump* of the stereo. It matched the *thump, thump, thump* of her heart. She had a headache. The parrot squawked, regarding her, head to one side, with its bright, beady eyes. It squawked again, a shrill, ear-piercing demand for attention.

"You do that one more time," she said, "and I'll chop off your head."

On the counter Baba looked up at her reproachfully from the cover of *Forgiveness.* She'd left the book there after speed-reading a chapter following an argument with Emmy earlier.

She regarded the parrot. "I didn't mean what I just said. I'm sorry. Really. I know you're hungry. I'd squawk, too." She walked to the hallway. "Did you clean Deanna's cage?" she called.

But, of course, Emmy couldn't hear her over the stereo. She went back to the kitchen and fed the parrot. Deanna was a green Amazon. Emmy had wanted her so desperately that she'd promised to stop asking whether she could, please, use makeup like everyone else she knew. In the three months since Deanna had taken up residence in the corner of the kitchen, the parrot had heard Daisy nag Emmy so often that it had started squawking, "Clean the damn cage."

Emmy appeared in the kitchen. "What's for dinner?"

"Heat up the soup if you're starving, otherwise wait till I get home. I'll do that baked chicken and potato thing you like."

Amalia was always telling her that she should get Emmy to cook for herself, which was true. But food, good food, was a big deal with her, and she enjoyed cooking for other people. As a child, she'd grown to endure the weird combinations her father had mixed up like the paints in his artist's palette. Broccoli with maple syrup, eggs scrambled with cranberry sauce. He didn't like being bound by convention; just because salmon wasn't usually served sprinkled with powdered sugar was no reason why it couldn't be served that way. *"If you're hungry enough, you'll eat it."*

She glanced around for her keys. "I have to go meet Nicholas Wynne."

"Why d'you say it like that?" Emmy had hopped up onto the counter and was swinging her legs. *"Nicholas Wynne,"* she said, imitating Daisy's voice.

"Isn't that his name?"

"Yeah, but when you go to Kit's, you don't say, 'I have to go meet Kit Niemeyer.'"

"Well, it's different."

"How?"

"Emmy, don't bug me, okay? I've got stuff on my mind."

"Want a peanut?" Deanna inquired. "Want some toast?"

"And you've got to start feeding her," she said, with a glance at the parrot which was hanging upside down from her perch. "It's not fair to leave it all to me."

"Did Dad talk to you about me living with him?" Emmy said, her voice elaborately casual.

Daisy's hand tightened around her purse, but she forced herself to remain calm. She figured Emmy had probably been rehearsing the words for some time. "He said he was going to," Emmy added.

"Well, he didn't," she said carefully. This topic came up periodically, usually after they'd disagreed about something, and then it was dropped. She was fairly certain Emmy had no wish to live with her father, fairly certain, in fact, that it was mutual—Toby didn't want a fourteen-year-old daughter cramping his lifestyle. Still, she had a knot in her stomach.

"He said he was going to," Emmy repeated, popping a grape into her mouth. "He *promised*."

Daisy glanced at the clock. She was going to be late. She looked at her daughter. "What's the reason this time?"

Emily sighed. "I've told you like a hundred times.

It's only fair. You've had me for fourteen years. Now it's his turn."

"Quit banging your feet against the cabinet," Daisy snapped. "And get down off the counter. What's another reason?"

"He has air-conditioning in his apartment?"

The question mark at the end of the sentence and the faint smile on her daughter's face told Daisy this wasn't anything to lose sleep over, but she felt irritated anyway. Last week, Toby had asked her for a loan because the brakes had gone on his truck and one of his fillings had come loose, so he'd had to fork out money for the dentist and he was coming up short on the rent. But he'd pay her back, no problem.

She suspected him of putting Emmy up to this. She should call his bluff.

"Emmy." She studied her daughter. "Maybe it seems like nothing to you when you talk about wanting to live with your father, but it gets me right here." She poked a finger at her chest. "I know we've been fighting a lot lately and I'm not always the easiest person to live with, but I love you and I honestly try my best…." Her nose stung with tears and, not wanting to win a sympathy concession from Emmy, she just stopped. In an instant, Emmy was off the counter, her arm around Daisy's shoulder.

"I'm sorry, Mom. I love you."

"I love you too, sweetie, more than anything else

in the world. And don't be sorry. You have a right to feel the way you do."

"It's just that Dad asked me to ask you."

Daisy kept her mouth shut. I am going through a difficult time right now, she told herself as Emily walked her to the truck. But adversity tests character.

Still, it wasn't the perfect frame of mind for meeting her father's biographer. And she probably shouldn't have worn a shirt that proclaimed, Doesn't Play Well With Others.

Deep breaths. She started the ignition. *Everyone comes into our lives for a reason*, Baba said. Maybe Nicholas Wynne had come into her life to teach her tolerance. His job in the cosmic universe was to be the fly in her serenity. She would be firm, calm and polite. But there would be no biography.

His hair damp from the shower, Nick took a look at his clothes, lined up on hangers and still slightly wrinkled from their transatlantic voyage. Linen this, cotton that. Served him right he supposed for refusing to buy synthetics. He'd got most of the things on vacation in Nice last year and brought them, thinking they looked somewhat Californian. Now, inspecting himself as he left the apartment, he could see that they didn't. Pity.

Out on the street, he eyed the never-ending flow of traffic on Pacific Coast Highway, waited for a lull, then made a dash for it. As he reached the other side, he heard the screech of brakes and a hurled epithet from one of the vehicles. Assuming it had been directed at him, he turned toward the road. As he did, a flurry of movement caught his eye. He looked down to see a small, bedraggled and trembling white dog.

He squatted beside it and felt around for broken bones.

"Idiots like you shouldn't be allowed to have animals," a woman called out from the open window of a battered gray truck that had stopped for a red light. "You're lucky it wasn't killed."

The woman's pale oval face was partially obscured by a lot of long red hair, but he didn't have to see her expression to know that she was angry. "It isn't my dog," he said politely, his hand still on the dog's back. "But if I locate its owner, I'll pass along your sentiments." Bad-tempered shrew.

"You need to keep him on a leash," the woman yelled.

"You need a leash around your neck," Nick muttered, and then the light turned green and the truck roared out of sight, long hair trailing like a ribbon through the window. He checked the dog's neck. No collar. It licked his hand. Now that he'd taken a better look, the dog was probably the ugliest little animal he'd ever seen.

The dog licked Nick's hand again.

"Don't get attached," Nick said.

CHAPTER SIX

"LOOK," DAISY MUTTERED to the waitress, "I'm not here, okay? This guy with an English accent is going to come in and ask for me but I'm not here."

"Huh?"

"Long story. I nearly killed a dog and I'm too shaken up to talk right now, and I don't really want to talk to him anyway, so just tell him I'm not here."

"Is he, like, a boyfriend, or something?"

"God, no. I've never even met him—"

"Then how do you—"

"Leah." She grabbed the waitress by the shoulders. "*Puh-lease*. I'm not here. What you see is a figment of your imagination."

Leah, slowly shaking her head, left the kitchen. Daisy turned back to the crème brûlées. Her hands were still trembling from the near miss with the dog, and she was overdue for a showdown with Toby over the money he was spending. She felt too scattered to break the news to Nicholas Wynne that the biography was off. No. Avoidance was the only way out.

As she finished the desserts, she remembered she had to pick up Emmy from school. She peered through the serving window that opened into the dining room and saw a youngish guy sitting alone, his back to her. Could that be him? A bald guy talking to the hostess? Nicholas Wynne? Maybe. Damn. She was stuck in the back of the restaurant with no escape route. Thankfully, Toby wasn't around—they'd run out of heavy cream and he'd gone down to the corner market for more—or she'd have to deal with him, too. Think, she commanded her brain. Her glance fell on the torch she'd been using. Sacrificing one of the crème brûlées, she scorched it until it began to smoke. Then to speed things along, she lifted it up just under the detector, which obligingly began to screech. For good measure, she yelled "fire" and dropped a pan on the floor. Three of the wait staff ran into the kitchen and in the ensuing commotion she slipped out of the restaurant.

"THIS IS SO WEIRD," the waitress told Nick. "She was here five minutes ago, and now she's gone."

The woman looked like Cameron Diaz, actually every other woman in Laguna Beach looked like Cameron Diaz or at least Cameron Diaz, Laguna version. She was very pretty, of course, and wore black trousers and a white shirt, her hair tied up in a ponytail. Her name, she'd already told him, was

Leah. He had no idea whether she was lying about Daisy. In any case, it was fairly evident that even if he forcefully restrained Daisy in the kitchen, he couldn't make her talk.

"Just vanished into thin air, eh?"

Leah smiled. "You have a really cute accent."

Nick smiled back. "Thank you. In England, though, nobody thinks twice about it. Back there, people would be telling you that you have a cute accent."

"Wow." One hand went to her hair. "Hey, you know who you look like? Anthony Bourdain."

"Never heard of him," Nick said. "You look like Cameron Diaz."

Leah squealed and slapped his arm. "Get *out*."

"I'm serious," he assured her, but vanity had reared its ugly head. "Who *is* Anthony Bourdain?"

"He's this guy on the Travel Channel."

"The Travel Channel." This rang a bell. "Is he the one who eats snakes?"

"Yeah, he eats all this disgusting food like snake hearts and stuff, and he's a celebrity chef at some restaurant in New York."

"Snake hearts?" Daisy might have just slipped around the corner, he theorized. If he killed a few more minutes, maybe she would reappear, thinking the coast was clear. "God, how ghastly. What else?"

Leah glanced around, obviously not wanting to ruin the appetites of other diners. "Maggots."

He nodded. "Actually, maggots are quite delicious, prepared properly, that is. I rather like them on toast. With a cup of cocoa."

Leah studied him. "You do not."

"You're right. Cocoa imparts an odd flavor, much better with beer."

Leah was still eyeing him closely. "He even wears his hair in a ponytail like yours. *And* he's tall and he's got this look like he's up to no good."

Nick started to speak, but the front door had opened and a young woman was standing in the doorway uncertainly—as Daisy no doubt would if she thought he might be hanging around. But then another woman jumped up from her seat. "Connie," she said. "Over here."

He turned his attention back to Leah. "Up to no good?" He feigned dismay. "You're not suggesting—"

"No, I just meant he was kind of, well you know…dark and kind of devilish…" Her face turned scarlet. "Listen, I gotta go. Can I get you some dessert?"

Nick considered, then decided Daisy probably wasn't coming back. He paid for his meal and then a thought struck him. He strolled back to the kitchen where he caught a glimpse of the sort of controlled chaos that seemed the norm in restaurant kitchens—at least the ones he'd seen on TV. A couple of male chefs, stirring pots; waitresses balancing plates. He motioned to Leah, who had just picked up a plate of artistically arranged scallops and asparagus all tarted up with thin strips of something red.

"Hi," she said, as though they hadn't just spent ten minutes chatting to each other. "What's up?"

"I was just wondering what Daisy looked like?"

"You've never met her?"

"Actually, I haven't." *Well, yes, I know her intimately*, he stopped himself from saying, *which is why I'm asking*. "Seems odd, I know, but…" He shrugged. No big deal, as Leah would probably say.

"Okay." She regarded the scallops for a moment. "She's kind of short, and she has long red hair, and she always wears, like, these peasant clothes? And she's got a whole bunch of T-shirts with stuff on the front. Weird sayings and stuff."

"Such as?"

"Well, like yesterday, she had one that said, I Just Do What The Voices Inside My Head Tell Me."

Nick smiled. Pity they wouldn't tell her to talk to him.

"Weird, huh? And, oh yeah, she has freckles and she sometimes wears these big straw sun hats with ribbons on them. She looks kind of like an artist, but she's not."

"No?"

Leah shook her head. "No, mostly she just cooks…she makes the desserts for this place and she looks after goats."

"I see." He smiled. "And the goats…where would they be?"

She gave him an appraising look. "Are you, like, an old boyfriend of hers or something?"

"No, no. Nothing like that. Just—"

"Sure," she said, as though he'd answered her question. "Well, anyway, she lives off Laguna Canyon Road somewhere. I've never been there, but I hear she's got this big field or something with log cabins and that's where she lives. With the goats."

"I see." He nodded at the plates in her hand. "Right, then. Better get that out there, before it gets cold."

THAT NIGHT, he drove up to L.A. to visit a screen-writer friend who had moved to the States a few years back. Inevitably, the talk moved on to Nick's current project, which seemed to be sputtering.

"Well, even when I spoke to her from England I wouldn't say she was wildly enthusiastic," he said. "Truman's brother was all for it, though, as was the widow. But just about the time I arrived, she had an accident. The widow. Fell out of a dune buggy."

"Good heavens. And she's Truman's widow? How old is she?"

"Late sixties, I think. I haven't met her. Anyway, I finally reached Daisy on the phone. She was less than enthusiastic, but she agreed to meet me. And didn't show up."

"Hmm. Wonder what's going on?"

"I don't know, but quite frankly it's annoying. If she doesn't want to talk, I'd prefer that she just tell me instead of playing coy."

TOBY STOKED THE BRICK oven with the last of the apple branches and slammed the door shut. He had an idea for this dish with blackened pork that he wanted to put on the menu, but he couldn't keep his mind on what to serve with it because of the way things were going with Daisy. She might deny it, but the place would be nothing without him—the *Orange County Register* had even written a review: "A Rising Young Star in the Orange County Culinary Scene." But the way things were going, he wasn't doing his best work and something had to give before she drove everyone crazy.

"Hey." Leah touched his arm. "Pay me some attention."

Toby put his arms around her. She wasn't supposed to be hanging around in the kitchen before her shift, but she'd stopped by anyway and he wasn't about to turn her away. "I'm sorry, babe, I got a lot on my mind."

"Like what?"

"Stuff. Daisy. She's on my back like you wouldn't believe." He told her about the whole salamander thing. How Daisy was the one who wanted him to order it, then how she made him look like an idiot when he tried to and then how she changed her mind again and said it was okay. "I mean, how am I supposed to do my job, when she's like this total head case?"

"What is it? Emmy giving her a hard time?"

He shook his head. "She and Emmy fight all the time, but that's pretty much normal." He hauled a stainless steel bin of carrots from the cold storage room, set them on the counter. "There's this guy from England who's supposed to be writing a biography of her old man and she's making some big deal out of it—"

"From England? I bet that was the guy who came in here a few nights ago. I served him. Daisy hid in the kitchen."

Toby rolled his eyes. He started chopping the carrots. "See, that's what I mean. She's acting like a nutcase."

"Why doesn't she want to talk to him?" Leah smiled. "He's cute."

"That Nick guy?" Toby set down the knife and turned to look at her. "You think *he's* cute?"

Leah laughed. "Don't go getting all jealous. You're *way* cuter."

Toby grinned. It was obvious that Leah dug him. She lived in this really cool apartment on the Balboa Peninsula, but her roommate had just moved out so

Leah was hinting around that maybe he should move in, which was perfect as far as he was concerned. Except that with the way Daisy was these days, he didn't want her going to pieces on him—even though she always claimed she didn't care who he dated.

"You know what though?" Leah came over to stand next to him. "I bet if Daisy met him, she'd like him. I mean, he's a nice guy. Couldn't you could just call him and explain how things are with her? Like she's kind of…sensitive?"

"I talked to him already." He turned back to the carrots. "What else am I supposed to say?"

Leah put her arms around his waist, leaned her face against his back. "You're smart, you can come up with something. If Daisy talks to him, she's off your back." She pressed a little closer. "Which is win-win, right? Hey, maybe she'll go for him or something."

"Daisy?"

"Yeah. Why not? She'd be kind of cute if she fixed herself up."

"He's not Daisy's type." Toby brought the knife down on a line of carrots. He couldn't see Daisy with any other guy, especially some English dude with a pony tail. "Quit that." He pushed Leah's hands away from his belt. "I got work to do. You better go—I'll catch you later."

But after Leah left, he started thinking about what

she'd said. It couldn't hurt to just call and fill Nick in on Daisy. Let the guy know that she didn't do stress real well—as he knew better than anyone. He'd be doing everyone a favor, right? He went over to the desk and flipped through the stack of business cards in the desk drawer, found Nick's and dialed the number. He tapped his fingers, waiting for the guy to pick up.

"Nick Wynne here."

"Hey. Toby Fowler, Daisy's ex-husband. We talked the other day."

"Oh, right. Yes. How are you?"

"Fine. How's it going for you?"

"Um…well I'm a bit frustrated actually. Funny thing you should call. I was going to give you a ring. It's about Daisy—"

"She's giving you the runaround?"

"You could say that. Any suggestions?"

"Not off the top of my head, but if you wanna come over here maybe we can talk about it some more, see what we can work out."

"Right." Toby heard the sound of papers rustling. "What time would be convenient for you?"

"You name it," Toby said. "I'm here every day— well, Mondays we're closed but every day, except Monday, from about noon till around eleven. Depending on business. Come before four, that's when things get crazy. We start serving dinner at five." He glanced at his watch. Five minutes to two. "If you wanna come over right now, that would work."

"Right." A pause. "Um, as a matter of fact, I was on my way over a few days ago—to meet Daisy actually—when this bloody dog narrowly escaped becoming flattened by a lorry."

"A dog?" Something clicked in Toby's brain. "What time, do you remember?"

"I don't know exactly. Late afternoon."

Toby grinned. Had to be the one Daisy nearly hit. Some pretty big coincidence, if you asked him. Maybe it was like a sign or something. "Dog's okay now, though?"

"The dog? Oh fine, fine. Driving me batty but all right otherwise. I've got it in my apartment, as a matter of fact. Ugly thing. I'd take it to the animal shelter, but it's so bloody piteous, no one would have it and then I'd have its death on my conscience."

"Stuff happens," Toby said, finding it hard to imagine feeling guilty about a damn dog, an ugly one to boot. "Can't get hung up on it." And then he had an idea. "You know what? Daisy might be willing to take the dog."

"D'you think so?"

"She's a sucker for animals. Especially if they're ugly."

"Well, this one certainly is."

"How many legs?"

"Legs? Well four—"

"Daisy's got a three-legged dog and a cat with no tail. The weirder the better."

"This one has an enormous head and a scrawny body. No one in their right mind would want it."

"Perfect for Daisy then."

"So you're suggesting—"

"I'm suggesting that if she's giving you the runaround, this is a foolproof way to meet her. She comes down to rescue the poor puppy and, wow, look who just happens to be here, too?"

"So…um, should I just bring the dog with me?"

"Sure." Then he remembered the Health Department. "Wait, you can't have dogs in restaurants. Just stop by anyway, we'll come up with something to tell Daisy once she gets here."

"Right, well—"

"I'll give her a call. See you in a few."

Toby hung up the phone and called Daisy. For once she answered the damn thing. "Hey, Daze. There's this dog wandering around outside, no collar. Looks like someone abandoned him."

She sighed. "God, what is wrong with people?"

"Dunno. Think maybe you could take it, though?"

Another sigh. "I'll be right down."

"Hold on." He estimated the time it would take for the biographer to walk over. "Uh, this girl took it out for a walk, I told her to take her time. So why don't you come by in, say, an hour? Maybe a little less…say forty-five minutes or so?"

If this worked, he decided as he returned to dinner preparations, he owed Leah a night out on the town. Win-win all around.

"THAT WAS TOBY," Daisy told Uncle Martin as she hung up. "A poor little dog somebody dumped off. I told him I'd come down and get it."

"You already have four dogs," Martin said.

She met his eyes. "Now I'll have five."

Martin stopped by a couple of times a week, sometimes to see Emmy, sometimes just to talk. He and Johanna lived in Monarch Bay, just south of town. Since Daisy had never known her mother—who had apparently abandoned her after giving birth—and her father hadn't exactly been father-of-the-year material, Martin and Johanna had been de facto parents. Martin more so than Johanna, who was one of those high-maintenance women who wore Manolo Blahniks, was allergic to animals and honestly couldn't understand why Daisy just didn't sell that damn hippy compound and buy a more suitable place to raise a fourteen-year-old daughter.

While Johanna tended to fling up her hands in exasperation, Martin was so doggedly conscientious that Daisy couldn't spend more than half an hour with him before she was practically gibbering.

Martin never dressed in anything less casual than a sport coat. Sometimes she'd look at his immaculate shirt cuffs and wonder what would happen if he went crazy one day and rolled one all the way to the elbow and let the other flop crazily around his wrist? The world would almost certainly cease to exist.

He glanced at his watch. "How did it go with the biographer?"

"It didn't."

"Weren't you supposed to meet him two days ago?"

"I nearly ran over a dog," Daisy said. "And I felt too frazzled to deal with him right then."

"But, of course, you called him to apologize and set up another meeting?"

His tone of voice and expression said that he knew damn well she hadn't.

"Martin, I'm really worried about Amalia. She's drinking again and her asthma's bad and…" She'd almost mentioned the dream, then thought better of it. "I really don't think the biography's a good idea."

"Why?"

"Because Amalia's already fragile."

"Let's stop using Amalia as an excuse," he said. "Why are *you* resisting?"

"I just think some things are better left unexamined."

Martin sighed. "I *was* hoping for something a tad more elucidating."

"Dad was too complex, too private. He wouldn't like being neatly packaged between the covers of a book. I mean, did *you* understand him? Really, understand him?"

"That's hardly the point. Biographies have been successfully written on very complex people. Einstein, for example—"

"We're talking about *my* father," Daisy said. "And you're asking me why I don't want it…"

"Go ahead then. Explain."

"I just think it's ridiculous to expect a stranger who never even met Dad to take all these different opinions and shape them into something that would even vaguely resemble him. It's like…like if I threw a bunch of different, unrelated ingredients—flour say, rose petals, ink and sugar—in the air and expected them to fall into a pan and become a cake."

THAT HADN'T satisfied Martin either, she thought as she drove to Wildfire to pick up the dog. Not surprisingly, because she had hardly scratched the surface of her objections to the biography. The thing was, what could you really do about the past anyway? It was over. The more you dug around in it, the more you thought about it. Better to just leave it alone, undisturbed.

A few minutes later, she parked in the small lot behind the restaurant and walked around to the front door. Wildfire was really Toby's baby: his dream to open a restaurant, his idea to smoke the salmon and albacore over natural woods, his menu. He'd been happy to turn over the design of it to her, though, and she'd spent a lot of time thinking about the way the place should look. It had all turned out pretty well—if she did say so herself and if she ignored her father's ever-present condemnation: "It's okay, but you could do better. Amateurish. Predictable."

"Quiet," she whispered, pausing as she always did, in the doorway. The tablecloths were the color of shallow ocean waves, pale, pale green and shot through with light. She'd looked everywhere for the fabric. The walls were a shade or two more intense. Filtered sunlight from the patio made the room seem like an underwater grotto. That was her intent anyway. Toby had suggested serving Dramamine with the main course.

She walked into the kitchen. A man was leaning against the wall where the menus and work schedules were pinned to a corkboard. A salesman talking to Toby, she thought, although he didn't exactly look like one. His face in three-quarter profile, struck her as vaguely...she searched for a word. Dangerous? No, too melodramatic. Sinister? No. His dark hair was drawn back into a ponytail, and he wore some sort of unstructured jacket. Black. Linen maybe, expensive definitely. Cream shirt. When he turned slightly, she saw a pale green silk tie, loosely knotted.

"Where's the dog?" she asked Toby, sensing something was up. Last week he'd tricked her into coming down to the restaurant telling her he needed to talk about Emmy. But when she'd got down there, he'd introduced her to this Realtor who wanted to buy her cabins. They'd given her this high-pressure sales pitch about how the land was worth millions, and Toby had complained about the freeloaders living there. The funny thing was that Martin was always complaining about Toby being a freeloader.

"If you're here about the property," Daisy said, "it's not for sale."

The guy laughed. Toby looked amused, too, but also a bit uncomfortable, which meant he was up to something.

"And we don't need another sala...sal—"

"Salamander," Toby said.

She put her hands on her hips. "The dog?"

Toby and the other man exchanged glances, and then something clicked.

"Wait. I've seen you before. You're the guy whose dog I nearly killed."

His eyes widened. "You're the woman in the truck, then? The one who called me an idiot?"

"Well, anyone who let a dog run loose—"

"It wasn't…isn't my dog. He sort of materialized at my feet as I was crossing the road…." He hesitated. "It's not exactly, well, appealing. Perhaps whoever owned him just got tired of looking at him."

Daisy stared at him. She'd heard that voice before. Things were beginning to click into place. "Where is the dog now?" she asked suspiciously.

"My apartment. Probably finishing the demolition job it started yesterday."

"*It?*"

"Well, I'm not sure whether it's a he or she."

"You didn't look?"

He laughed. "No, I can't say I did. It's…he or she is very shaggy and I, um, didn't think to look."

"You're not a dog person, are you?"

"Well, I wouldn't say that."

"Do you have a dog?"

"No, I—"

"Or a cat?"

"Not actually, I did once know a cat, sort of…"

"And now you want to get rid of the puppy?"

"Look, it's not that I have anything against dogs."

Daisy folded her arms across her chest. She'd walked right into a trap. She could either walk right out, or stick around to see how long Nicholas Wynne would keep up his little game.

"The thing is, I'm staying in an apartment that

doesn't allow animals and your husb…Toby here suggested that you were very fond of animals…"

"He couldn't bring it over here," Toby chimed in. "Health regulations."

Daisy nodded. Her father's biographer looked nothing like the tweedy, stout, red-veined-nose type she'd imagined. True, Margaret had described him as handsome, but Margaret had once confided that she found Rodney Dangerfield erotically attractive.

"It cried and barked all night. Finally, I had no option but to bring him into the bedroom. I've had to leave him locked up in the bathroom today though, so…look, we might as well get this over with." He extended his hand. "Nick Wynne. Good to meet you at last."

CHAPTER SEVEN

"VERY CLEVER," SHE SAID after Nicholas Wynne, finally realizing she wasn't going to shake his hand, had withdrawn it. "A trick to get me down here, huh?"

"He really does have this dog he needs to get rid of," Toby insisted.

The biographer at least had the grace to look embarrassed. Despite his European sophistication—she could imagine him drinking coffee at one of those outdoor Parisian cafes, or maybe at some hip wine bar in London—the idea of him tucking the puppy into bed was endearing. But the fact that he'd obviously colluded with Toby was not in his favor. She could just imagine Toby selling him the idea. "Dude, once she thinks you love dogs, she'll be putty in your hands."

We'll see about that.

Toby had turned his attention to the brick oven, feeding apple tree branches into its ever-hungry mouth. The kitchen was sweltering, and her face felt flushed and hot. Nicholas/Nick seemed unaffected, cool and composed in his stylish clothes. Although she wasn't the type to sneak peeks at herself in every reflective surface she happened upon, she felt a sudden need for a reassuring glance. On second thought, it was better not to know. The wind had done a number on her hair, which on good days was reddish-blond and curly and on not-so-good days bore a faint resemblance to the coat of a mongrel mix with terrier in its genes. That morning she'd pulled on a tatty, blue cotton skirt and a faded, black top—what the hell did this one say? She couldn't remember without glancing down at her breasts.

Think.

"Toby." She addressed her ex-husband, who was now arranging pork tenderloins onto a metal rack and making a big pretense of being too absorbed in what he was doing to listen. "Emmy needs a ride home from school. You need to leave right now."

"Why can't she ride the bus?" Toby asked, clearly reluctant to leave.

"Because I was going to pick her up and we…were going to look at surfboards," she said, improvising rapidly. "And she wanted to check out this new video store in Newport Plaza. Go." She grabbed his keys from the rack where he always hung them. "Tell her I'll see her later. Drive carefully."

"No, Daisy, I think I'll drive like a maniac." His face dark, Toby snatched the keys from her outstretched hand, nodded at Nick and left.

WELL, WELL, WELL, Nicholas thought as he and Daisy warily eyed each other in the kitchen, neither quite sure what move to make next. So this is *Innocence* all grown up.

He smiled. She had amazing skin—dewy, there was no other word for it, and her hair tumbled around her shoulders. In the theatre of his mind, he had cast her as a kitchen wench; probably because they were standing in a kitchen with a bloody great brick oven, in which you could easily shove a cow, maybe a couple of pigs, too. She wore a long cotton skirt and a shirt that proclaimed, This Was Not The Day I Ordered. Please Bring Me Something Else.

"What sort of day did you order?" he asked, after the silence had lingered for a moment or two.

She shrugged. "Look, I might as well come right out and say it. I'm not going to talk about my father. Maybe I didn't make it clear enough. I thought I did, but…well, you're here, so maybe I didn't. I'm sorry you had to come all this way to hear that, but I don't know what else to say."

"Nothing else *to* say," Nick reassured her, thinking of the red ribbon of hair that had trailed through the open window of her truck yesterday. Today, her hair looked more ginger than red. Or was it copper? "Plenty of other people for me to talk to, you know. Besides, spending November in the

Laguna sunshine, as opposed to shivering back in London…" He smiled again, endearingly, he hoped. He would come up with a defense later. For now, it was enough that she was actually there in front of him. "Well, it isn't exactly a hardship."

"The thing is, he was a very private man," Daisy said, as though Nick hadn't spoken. "And complicated, too. He wouldn't have wanted someone poking around in his life, trying to figure out what made him tick."

"Can't say I blame him at all," Nick said. "Or you. My own family certainly has its share of dotty characters. An auntie given to dancing naked under the full moon."

Daisy's pale green eyes narrowed suspiciously.

"Honestly. I was thrashed once for spying on her through my bedroom window."

"Thrashed? You mean beaten?"

"Well, not exactly." He didn't want to give her the wrong idea, although he supposed if it generated sympathy for him… "It was sort of a figure of speech."

"*Did* you spy on your aunt?"

"I did." He made a mental note never to say anything else to Daisy Fowler unless he was fully prepared to defend it. "But the thrashing I received was more of the…verbal variety."

"So you exaggerated?"

"I suppose you could say that."

"So what if *I* said my father thrashed me? How would that look in print?"

Nick took a breath. Sweat beaded on his brow. He hadn't noticed until now how bloody hot the kitchen was. And the damn fire was roaring away as though it was midwinter. "What about some fresh air?" he asked. "Shall we walk over and see the dog?"

"You know what?" Daisy smiled faintly, signaling perhaps that she wouldn't press him for an answer to her question. "When I sent Toby off, he was right in the middle of prepping for tonight's dinner. I can't go anywhere until he gets back." She took a glass from one of dozens stacked on an aluminum shelf, filled it with water from the tap and handed him a glass. "Here. You look as though you're about to melt."

"Thanks." Nick drank the water and immediately felt better. "Mind if I stay and talk?"

"What about the puppy?"

"The puppy." Nick was beginning to dislike the puppy. He thought about it again. Well, actually, it wasn't a bad little thing. "The puppy," he said again. "Well, I should think it would be all right for a while longer."

She narrowed her eyes. "You're sure? He has plenty of water? Food?"

"Filet mignon," Nick said.

"Oh, come on. Even I don't feed my dogs filet mignon."

"Mr. Barko," he said. "Bought the bag this morning. Chicken flavor."

"I don't mean to give you a bad time."

He felt a faint ray of hope. "Not at all."

"Actually, I really, *really* appreciate you being so understanding about this whole biography thing,"

Nick just smiled.

"It's weird how you can pick up…I don't know, vibes. I should have met you first thing. I could have saved myself about ten pounds."

"Sorry?" Nick said, not entirely sure he'd understood.

"I was obsessing. People kept calling me—people you'd interviewed—telling me I should talk to you. And I just started getting more and more frustrated, and when that happens—" she shot him a sideways glance "—I eat."

"Do you?" Nick said, eager to grasp the conversational straw. "My…a woman I know in England, complains that she loses her appetite completely whenever she's upset."

"Women like that make me ill."

Nick decided that he rather liked Daisy. It was early, of course, and she could still prove difficult and uninformative, but there was something refreshingly straightforward about her—other than the week she'd spent avoiding him.

"Is this your girlfriend?" Daisy asked.

"Sorry?"

"The woman who doesn't eat." She laughed. "I just figured if you knew her eating habits, you had to know her pretty well."

"Yes, well…" He thought about Valerie. The night before he had left for California, he walked over to her Finsbury Park flat, a mile or two away from his own, with the intention of ending the relationship. It hadn't quite happened. "She's not actually, well I suppose you could call her, but—"

Daisy laughed, a big honking snort of a laugh. "That tells me all I need to know. So what's her name?"

"Her name?"

"Your not really a girlfriend."

"Um, Valerie."

Daisy nodded as though this was an important character revelation.

"She had this cat," he said just for something to say. "Valerie did. His name was Chairman Meow. Horrible cat. Enormous and cantankerous."

"You're not a cat person, either?"

"No, I'm not. A cat climbed into my cot when I was a baby. I don't remember this, of course, my mother told me, but I've never liked them much since. Valerie's cat was particularly loathsome. Malevolent. I had the distinct suspicion that he knew every rotten thing I was thinking about him and, more ominously, was filing it away for future reference."

"He probably was," Daisy said. "So, did a dog climb in your crib too?"

"Sorry?" A moment passed, then enlightenment dawned. "Oh, I see. It's not exactly that I don't like dogs, actually I don't mind them, it's just that my present circumstances—"

"What happened to Chairman Meow?"

"He was hit by a London taxi."

"Oh." Daisy's hand flew to her mouth. "Did he…"

"Unfortunately, yes."

In fact, the cat's sudden death had been the reason he hadn't called things off with Valerie that night. While he was ringing Valerie's doorbell, Chairman Meow was a few houses down, sauntering into the path of the taxi. He'd heard the screech of tires and gone to investigate. Valerie had found him cradling her dying cat.

"We buried him in Valerie's courtyard," he told Daisy. "Beneath some geraniums. Valerie recited T.S. Eliot over the grave."

"'Growltiger's Last Stand.'"

Nick looked at her amazed. "Exactly. How did you—"

"I used to read T.S. Eliot to my daughter," she said. "Growltiger would seem like a good choice. 'One ear was somewhat missing…'" she said, "'…no need to tell you why, / And he scowled upon a hostile world from one forbidding eye.'"

"Remarkable," Nick said. He wouldn't have been able to recall the words on a bet. What he had remembered thinking that night, as he'd stood under the bucketing rain, was that he'd felt too drained for more melodrama.

But now, to sustain this tenuous connection he'd made with Daisy, he began dredging his memories for further examples of his love and compassion for four-legged things. There wasn't much to work with.

AS HE DROVE TO Emmy's school, Toby was seething. The whole thing with Daisy and the biographer had backfired and he had no one to blame but himself. He should have stayed out of it. And where did she get off, talking to him like he was the hired help and practically forcing him out of his own restaurant?

He slammed on the brakes—some old fart had stepped off the sidewalk, not even checking first—then he honked the horn. "Watch where you're going, why don't you?" he yelled out of the window. *Jerk*.

Not that he was jealous—hell, Leah was a lot cuter than Daisy—but he didn't like the way Nick had looked at her. He knew that look. The guy was supposed to be a biographer. Maybe he should call and explain the way things were with him and Daisy.

They might be divorced, but Daisy depended on him. Okay, not for money and stuff like that, but who had been there for her after the old man died? They'd been through a lot together. Maybe that was something Mr. Biographer needed to know.

Maybe he'd do the guy a favor, fix him up with one of the waitresses. Hot California chicks, who wouldn't want one?

He pulled into the parking lot of Emmy's school. Girls strolled around the campus like they owned the place. Girls with hair down to there and legs up to here, and all he could think about was dumb Daisy.

A bunch of kids burst through a side entrance. He spotted Emmy and honked. All the kids looked over at him, then Emmy recognized the truck and ran over. She looked kinda like Daisy. Long hair, except hers was dark like his. And she had eyes like a cat. Daisy's eyes.

"Where's Mom?" Emmy said through the open passenger window.

"Hi to you, too. You lucked out and got me instead. Pretend you're happy."

She shot him a look, unhooked her backpack from her shoulders and climbed into the truck. "So, where is Mom?"

"At the restaurant, talking to the biographer."

Emmy scooted around on the seat to look at him. "She's *talking* to him?"

"Yep." Toby maneuvered the truck through the traffic that was now starting to pour into the parking lot, and drove slowly through the hilly side streets around the school. He was hoping Emmy wouldn't insist on Newport Plaza, he wanted to just spend some time with her. Emmy was still looking at him. Amazed, like he'd just told her pigs could fly.

"*Finally.*"

"Yeah, well, I set it up."

"Wow." She had one foot tucked under her on the seat. "What'd you do?"

"I just made her see she was acting stupid, avoiding him the way she's been doing. I got him to come down to the restaurant and introduced them to each other."

"Cool," Emmy said. "I've been trying to think of some way to get her to meet him. He keeps calling and I feel sorry for him. He's just doing his job."

Let's hope that's all he's doing, Toby thought. He honked at some old woman in a Lincoln Continental who was driving along at ten miles an hour, rubber necking and holding up traffic as if she was the only one on the road.

"Open that window, will you?" he said without taking his eyes from the road.

She rolled it down a crack. "Mom is *so* impossible lately."

"What about now?"

"She's always making a big deal out of nothing. Like I lost my match last week, and she acts like it's the worst thing that could possibly happen, like it was some major disaster. And then she gets all hurt because I don't want to go to the ice-cream place with her. I've told her fifty million times I hate ice cream, but she thinks it's this magic stuff."

"That was it?" Toby was disappointed. "What else?"

"Nothing. She wanted me to go out to dinner with her and Uncle Martin, but Kelsey's mom took me home with her."

"Your Uncle Martin's got lots of money, kiddo," Toby said. "You *should* be nice to him." Except that he wouldn't blame her for not being nice. Martin was a pain in the ass, a pompous stuffed shirt who was always trying to cause trouble between him and Daisy.

"So I should be nice to him just because he's got lots of money?"

"No *just* because." She grinned. Her voice right then had sounded just like Daisy's. "But money never hurts."

"Are we going to the mall?"

"You want to?"

"*Ye-es*," she said, stretching the word into two syllables, making it sound like he'd asked the stupidest question in the world.

Toby sighed. Fine for Daisy to take her to the mall and buy whatever Emmy set her eyes on. Daisy had money. *He* got paid according to how well Wildfire was doing—Daisy's idea. If he spent money on equipment, it affected the bottom line. Translation, he got less money. Like the whole thing with the salamander. He'd had to explain about four times that it was this high-tech broiler, and if she wanted them to keep getting good press then she'd better quit bugging him about every damn dollar he spent

Even if Daisy blew, say, a thousand bucks a day, she couldn't spend all the money her father left her. But she pinched pennies until they screamed. And who was supposed to pay for this damn surfboard she'd sent him off to buy? He tried to remember if he had anything left on his personal credit card.

"What's wrong, Dad?"

"Nothing." Nick had money. The watch he was wearing probably cost about the same as the salamander Daisy had bitched about. "Nothing at all. Life's just one big hoot, right?"

"Come on." She fixed him with her Daisy-green eyes. "I know there is. Tell me."

"D'you talk to your mom about coming to live with me?"

Now it was Emmy's turn to sigh. "Yeah, but it made her sad…."

Toby nodded like he understood. *Can't have Mommy being sad, can we?* The truth was that he did kind of want Emmy to come and live with him. She was a cool kid and he loved her a whole bunch. Also, Daisy would have to give him more money for expenses. Even better still would be if he and Daisy got back together. He'd be on easy street for sure. But he didn't think Daisy would go for it.

"Something's wrong," Emmy said. "I'll keep bugging you until you tell me."

Toby laughed despite himself. Mostly Emmy took after him, but every so often, she was pure Daisy. "I'm worried about your mother."

"How come?"

"I don't know…I don't want to see her get hurt."

"Huh?"

"This Nick character. She takes one look at him and I might as well be on another planet for all she cares."

"What did she do?"

"Nothing, yet. But I'm thinking it wasn't such a good idea to get the two of them together."

She turned in the seat to look at him. "*Why?*"

"Something about him I don't trust."

"Like what?"

"He's too…I don't know. Smooth. And your mom's pretty naïve about people."

"Oh, she'll be okay." Emmy reached for her backpack. "Hey, can we stop at Super Slurp? I'm thirsty."

"Yeah, I guess." Toby pulled into the mini mall parking lot, handed over four of the quarters he kept in the ashtray and watched his daughter disappear into the store. It wouldn't hurt to tell her to watch out for her mother. To let him know if Nick started coming over to the house or something.

They ended up skipping the mall, and when he got back to Wildfire, Daisy and Mr. Biographer were so deep in talk, they didn't even hear him come in.

CHAPTER EIGHT

"BEING A FATHER is a part of my life where I feel…like a failure, quite frankly," Nick was telling Daisy. "I know Bella deserves more from me and I try, but she knows and I know that I'm a pretty miserable excuse for a dad…"

"Maybe you're being too hard on yourself," Daisy said. "That's kind of what parents do. I go into these fits of guilt over things I should have done for Emily, or shouldn't have done, and usually it turns out that she's fine…."

She heard a movement at the kitchen entrance and looked up to see Toby.

"Wow, you're back already?" She shook her head, coming out of Nick's story about his daughter to the realization that it was after four and she and Nick had been talking for God knows how long and Toby's expression was thunderous. "Hey, check this out." She pointed to the tray of gleaming, caramelized pork tenderloins on the counter. "Nick smoked them for you. And—" she waved at the containers of chopped bell peppers, all Christmassy green and red "—I did most of the prepping so you're pretty much all set."

Toby said nothing, just threw his keys onto the desk, pulled off his denim jacket, tossed it over the keys, removed his white chef jacket from the hook on the wall and, still without a word, grabbed one of the heavy aluminum pots hanging from an overhead rack. As he brought it to the counter, his arm hit a tub of peppers, knocking it to the floor. Pieces of red pepper scattered like confetti.

Daisy grabbed a handful of paper towels and started to clean up the spill, but Toby pushed her aside so roughly, she stumbled. In an instant, Nick was at her side, his hand extended.

"Thanks." She met his eyes briefly, then addressed Toby, who had gone for a broom and was sweeping with broad, ostentatious strokes and muttering under his breath. "Did you drop Emmy off at Kit's?"

"No." He kept sweeping.

She took a breath. His nose was out of joint and he was putting on a show for Nick. She didn't want to add to his little drama, but it was all she could do to restrain herself. "You want to tell me where, then?"

"She's at Leah's."

"Leah's?"

"Yeah, Leah's." He finished the cleanup, returned the broom to the closet, then walked over to the sink and washed his hands as meticulously as if he were preparing for brain surgery. "You need to talk to your daughter sometime, Daze," he said almost conversationally now. "See what she really thinks about things. See, Leah lives in a decent place with air-conditioning, not out on some dirt road with animals running around."

Daisy couldn't speak. For a moment, she almost forgot Nick. Toby, at the stove now, his back to her, was stirring something in a stock pot. Her heart was hammering so hard, it scared her. The time was coming, but this wasn't it.

A moment later, she was out on the sidewalk with no recollection of leaving the restaurant. Her face still burning, she leaned against the wall that divided Wildfire from the taco shop next door and tried to slow her breathing. Hot wind blew her hair, traffic rumbled by on Pacific Coast Highway. The afternoon light threw an amber glow over everything.

"I won't ask if you're all right." Nick was standing beside her, his shoulder almost touching hers. "One is never all right after something like that."

"Thanks," she said. "Meaning you've...?"

"Unfortunately, yes. And I can't even cast myself as the innocent party. Not in every instance, anyway."

"Sorry you had to witness it," Daisy said.

Nick shrugged. She felt it, the brush of his shoulder against hers.

"Probably why I'm a biographer," he said after a

moment. "Digging into other people's messes allows you to keep an objective distance. Not so easy to do when it's your own mess."

"*One's* own mess." Daisy turned her head to look at him. He smiled. A few moments passed. "Listen, about the puppy," she said. "I do need to go pick up Emmy and by the time we have dinner and she does her homework, it's going to be late. Can…it stay another night?"

"Of course."

"I'll call you in the morning, first thing," she said. "Oh wait, tomorrow's Saturday. Emmy has a tennis match. That should be over about eleven, okay?"

"No problem at all."

PROBABLY THE STUPIDEST four words he'd uttered all week, Nick decided ten minutes later, flat on his back on his kitchen floor, where he'd slipped in a puddle of pee.

"How on earth did you get out of the bathroom?" he asked the dog, who, overjoyed at his return, was running in little circles beside him, licking whatever bits of exposed flesh it could find. "You're a nuisance, you do know that?"

He pulled himself up off the floor, mopped up the mess, thinking as he did of Toby and wondering about Toby's relationship with Daisy. Jealousy would explain that performance. Humans were a strange lot when it came to affairs of the heart. As he himself knew quite well.

After he'd changed, he made himself a gin and tonic and carried it out to the balcony to watch the passing parade below. And think about Daisy. Had she been scared? Angry? He hadn't thought so then. She wasn't crying or hysterical—which was why he'd made that bloody stupid remark about why he wrote biographies.

Shallow and superficial. Keeps his subject at arm's length.

Restless, he carried the drink inside, held it in one hand as he paced. The puppy pounced at his bare feet, circling them and barking. His stepfather had been verbally abusive, not unlike Toby. Never any physical violence, but fright was a powerful weapon, and a loud, booming voice could be very threatening to a small child. Or a woman.

Acting on an impulse, he dialed Daisy's number and got her answering machine.

"It's Nick. Look…I feel, um, a bit awkward about saying this—it's probably none of my business, well…" He set his drink down on the kitchen counter, sorry now he'd started along this path. "Toby seemed very angry and volatile and, well, I wasn't exactly a pillar of strength…asinine comments and all that. You can probably tell I'm not very good at this sort of thing, but if, um, if you're feeling at all unsafe and you want someone to beat the bloody hell out of him—" the last few words came out in a rush "—actually I didn't mean that. Really just calling to see that you're all right."

His face flaming, he hung up the phone.

Later that evening, he had dinner with Martin at Las Brisas, a busy, trendy place with floor to ceiling windows that opened onto the oceanfront and, for an even closer Pacific dining experience, an outdoor patio with tall heaters to ward off the evening chill.

"I had a few words with my niece," Martin said, as soon as they'd sat down. "Has she contacted you yet?"

"We met this afternoon." He'd come prepared with a list of questions about Frank Truman, but somehow or other the conversation turned to Daisy's ex-husband.

"You've met him?" Martin's expression was inscrutable.

"Twice. Actually, he called me the second time. Daisy didn't want to talk and was there anything he could do."

He filled Martin in on the dog fiasco and stifled a yawn. The bloody dog had kept him awake again and he'd been forced to bring it into the bedroom where it had promptly jumped on the bed and relieved itself on the sheets.

"I'm taking the dog over to Daisy's tomorrow," he

said, with a glance at the open notebook to the side of his salad plate.

Martin rolled his eyes. "Daisy doesn't need another dog."

He motioned to the waiter, who was there immediately. A tall, blond surfer type who identified himself as Eric. Martin ordered a glass of merlot and glanced at Nick, who ordered a beer and hoped it wouldn't cause him to lapse into a soporific state.

"What was your impression of Toby?" Martin asked.

"A bit…volatile. Probably still has a thing for Daisy."

"Or her money," Martin said.

Nick waited.

"I'm sure he's fond of Emily and maybe Daisy too, but I doubt very much he'd still be around if Daisy hadn't inherited a substantial fortune. He's very clever, definitely has an eye out for himself. Daisy financed that restaurant. Without her, he'd be flipping burgers at a fast-food chain."

"What about Daisy?" Nick asked, realizing as he did that his interest wasn't entirely professional. "Why would she keep him around?"

"For the same reason she can't say no to a dog or the hippies on her property. She's very generous and openhearted, and people take advantage of her, her ex-husband being one of the biggest transgressors."

Nick thought again of the scene in the restaurant, sorry he wasn't the type to have swung a quick punch to the chef's jaw before making his exit. Like the black-hat cowboys in the TV westerns he'd watched as a boy. Tall, swaggering, lean-jawed and quick on the draw. If he succeeded in offing the bad guy, it would probably be through boredom.

"…and I'm hoping that at some point Daisy will just decide she's had enough of him," Martin was saying. "She's tough when she has to be. Toby knows he can only go so far." He tasted his wine, set the glass down again. "So when you met Daisy this afternoon…?"

"She doesn't want to talk about her father. Why do you suppose she's so against it?"

"Her misguided effort to protect Frank. In his last few years, Frank was in failing mental health, something Daisy denied then and probably still does."

DAISY HAD FOUND A MESSAGE from Nick waiting for her when she got home. She played it over several times and was playing it again when Kit dropped over to show her the quilt she was entering in the art festival.

"Listen to this," Daisy said, after she'd oohed and aahed over the quilt. As she rewound the tape, she realized she could recite Nick's words by heart.

"It's Nick. Look…I feel, um, a bit awkward about saying this…"

Daisy glanced at Kit's face as they listened, trying to judge her reaction as they listened and—this was really weird—ready to defend Nick.

She smiled at the bit about beating the bloody hell out of Toby. Not that she approved of physical violence—even upon Toby. It was just…sweet. Truthfully, she couldn't imagine Nick doing anything like that. Couldn't really imagine him losing his cool composure, which, she had to admit, she found rather attractive. Her father and then Toby had provided her with enough volatility to last a lifetime.

"Look at you grinning like a Cheshire cat," Kit said, clearly amused. "So you met him finally?"

"Yep."

"And it wasn't so bad?"

"Not bad at all." She hesitated. "But I didn't, you know, say anything about my father."

Kit curled up on the couch, pulling the afghan that Daisy kept draped over it down around her shoulders. "I want to hear all about it."

"Okay, first I have to tell you the really strange thing, though. That dog I told you I nearly killed? Guess whose it was."

"The biographer's?"

"Yep. Except not really. I mean it wasn't his dog."

"But it was the one Toby called you about?"

"Right." She frowned, remembering the strange way Toby had acted in front of Nick, almost like he was jealous, which made no sense since he was seeing Leah. "Remind me to tell you about Toby," she said. "First, though, I have to tell you about Nick."

"*Nick*." Kit smiled knowingly. "One day it's Nicholas Wynne, now it's Nick."

"Shut up." Daisy grinned back. "He told me to call him Nick. I mean, what am I supposed to call him? Come *on*."

"Okay, so anyway…" Kit prompted.

"So anyway, I went down to pick up this dog and, ta-da, the guy is the biographer."

"So he tricked you?"

"Yeah, well that's what I thought at first, which made me mad. But Nick—" she shot Kit a look "—Nick said he really did need to find a home for the dog, I guess it's so ugly, no one would want it—"

"You haven't seen it yet?"

"No. I'm going to pick it up tomorrow. But get this, when I told him I wasn't going to talk about my dad, he just shrugged and said 'fine.' I felt as though we were playing tug-of-war and the other side had just let go."

"He's biding his time," Kit said. "If you want my opinion, that is."

Daisy tossed a cushion at her. "Thanks for bursting my bubble."

"Not that you don't already know it on some level."

Daisy nodded. The thought had occurred to her, too. "Probably just trying to win my confidence, catch me off guard and then, pow, fire off the questions. Still."

"So what *did* you talk about?"

"Babies. I told him I volunteer at Children's Hospital, and he told me about his daughter and we could have gone on and on…except then Toby came in and started acting like a jerk."

Kit wove the fringe of the afghan between her fingers. "Daisy, you need to do something about Toby. Either get him out of your life or…"

"Or what?" She looked at Kit. "You're not going to suggest getting back together—trust me, there's no chance. He's Emmy's father and that's our only connection. And I want to help him get his life on track. I've got money and he hasn't. It's like—"

"Rescuing a puppy."

"Exactly."

"But a lot more trouble."

"Well, he doesn't pee on the rugs."

"True." Kit yawned and stretched. "It's getting late, I should take off."

"Want some hot chocolate first?" Daisy asked, pulling herself up off the couch when Kit nodded. In the kitchen, she ran water into the kettle and turned the burner on. "I feel a whole lot better now that I've met Nick," she called into the living room. "I just feel that I can deal with the biography, and I didn't think I could before."

"Good," Kit said.

"I'm even starting to think about whether I should just...feed him selected tidbits. 'My father?'" she drawled in a pseudo English accent. "'A lovely man. I had the most perfect childhood you could possibly imagine. Nothing but the best of everything was allowed in the house, the best music, the best poetry, the best books. I was never allowed to read comic books or to go to the movies. Toast and caviar for tea...lovely, *dahling*.'"

"Is that true?"

Daisy hesitated. She couldn't talk about this, not even with her best friend. "It's not *un*true."

"You really had caviar and toast for tea?"

"Yep." For tea, breakfast the next day, lunch, dinner, bedtime snacks. He'd wanted her to have the experience but, at God knows how much a pound, he wasn't about to waste one single egg. Even though he had millions of dollars, even though she'd gagged and thrown up at the table. "*Better get that tablecloth in the wash*," he'd said. "*It's going to stain.*"

"So what do you think about that?" she called, ignoring Kit's question. "Some carefully edited information?"

"Don't," Kit said.

"Don't what?"

"Don't think about what you should do. Don't

analyze it, don't do anything. Whatever happens will happen."

And of course there was Amalia to consider.

Back in the living room, Daisy looked at her friend, who was lying very still, her hands folded across her chest. Kit meditated every day and practiced yoga. When the subject of a biography had first come up, she'd lent Daisy a book called *Ten Simple Steps to Letting Go*. The first chapter seemed to have been written for her. "One minute we feel on top of the world, everything is chugging along just fine. And then, *boom!* Our life changes and we get clobbered."

That was exactly how she felt about the biography. But she'd been hoping for advice on what to do about it. And there was none. Basically, the book took about ten pages to say stuff happens, get over it.

She'd thrown the book across the room and made Wacky cake.

Kit meant well, though, it's just that sometimes she seemed to live on another planet. Daisy heard the kettle boil and went back into the kitchen, spooned chocolate into two cups, poured in the water, stirred and carried the drinks into the living room.

"Kelsey and I went on a hike up in Big Bear last year," Kit said, sitting up. "It was beautiful. Birds singing, sun shining through the trees. We were yakking away, feeling great. Then I looked up ahead and saw a bear on the path. I just stopped in my tracks. Kel did, too. My heart was thundering so hard, I thought the bear would hear it."

Kit blew across the steaming mug. "We both stood there for the longest time, I wanted to tell her that I'd distract it and for her to run, but I didn't want to alert the bear with any sound. And then it occurred to both of us at the same time that the bear wasn't moving. We both tiptoed a few steps down the path. Stopped. Peered. Still, the bear hadn't moved. And then Kelsey started laughing."

"It wasn't a bear?"

"No, it was a huge boulder on the path."

Daisy sipped her cocoa, waiting.

"The bear never existed, except in our minds," Kit said. "But we'd already made it a reality, complete with an escape plan." She cradled the mug between her hands and grinned at Daisy. "Maybe the biographer was your bear on the footpath."

"And Toby?"

"Toby *is* the bear."

DAISY WAS IN BED READING when the bear called later that night from the restaurant. She could hear the voices of the wait staff in the background, the clanking of pots.

"You talk to Emmy lately?"

"I talk to her all the time." She felt her body tense,

gearing for another battle. "Why?"

"She tell you she's embarrassed by you and all your hippy friends? She's fourteen, she goes to a school where all the other kids live in mansions—"

"If Emily is embarrassed by me, or by where she lives, she can tell me," Daisy said. "She doesn't need you to act as an intermediary."

"She doesn't want to hurt your feelings. She wants to live with me—"

"Bull."

"No, it's not bull. And another thing, if you want Wildfire to be a first-rate restaurant, you need to start laying out some cash."

CHAPTER NINE

"AND I THINK SHE *CARES* about you," Valerie's twin sister Gillian told Nick over drinks at a very dark Laguna bar. "It's just that she feels guilty about Richard, but as I've always told her, you can't base a relationship on guilt."

Nick stifled a yawn. He didn't want to offend Gillian, but it had been a very full day. Finally meeting Daisy, followed by dinner with her uncle, the sleepless night—thanks to the dog, who was probably making a meal of the couch cushions. And now drinks with Gillian, a flight attendant with a twenty-four hour layover in Los Angeles.

He fought another yawn. "Sorry. It's not the company."

Gillian, who looked enough like Valerie—a tall willowy, blue-eyed blonde—to make the evening even more surreal, smiled sympathetically. "Work?"

"Sort of." He thought of Daisy and his idiotic phone apology for his failure to defend her against her ex-husband in a way that, he imagined, would meet her father's approval. "I think I might take up karate," he said, surprising himself as much as Gillian with the remark.

She arched an eyebrow. "Would that come in handy with the biography, then?"

"Or what's that other thing, where you fling your opponent around—"

"Jujitsu?"

He nodded, absorbed by the idea.

"No," he said aloud.

"Not jujitsu? Well, what's that other thing…a studio just opened around—"

"Gillian," he said. "I'm just not the…how should I say it…the visceral type, am I? I mean words, not fists, are my weapons. I'm not a John Wayne or a…who? Charles Bronson. I'm—"

"Sloshed." She moved his drink to her side of the table. "That's it for you."

"I'm perfectly sober." He eyed the exotic, sweet drink he'd allowed her to talk him into ordering. "Although, I think I'd prefer a beer."

Gillian glanced at her watch. "My arm hurts where you twisted it."

Nick motioned to the cocktail waitress, ordered a beer for himself and another of the fruit salad concoctions for Gillian. "This biography I'm doing," he said after the waitress left. "Frank Truman…"

"The artist." She nodded. "Valerie's told me all about it. Problems with the daughter or something?"

Nick leaned back in his seat, folded his arms across his chest. "Daisy," he said. "I met her today."

Gillian waited. "And?"

And what? And he felt rather drawn to her? And acting on that feeling would almost inevitably disrupt progress. Although so far he'd made very little progress. And? He didn't know.

Gillian leaned slightly across the table. "Nick, are you all right? You seem odd."

"I think perhaps I'm having a midlife crisis."

She laughed. "You're forty-four."

"Five," he said. "That's midlife."

She still looked amused. "Why do you think you're having a crisis?"

He sighed. "An ever-expanding catalogue of failures. I'm an indifferent father, an unsupportive companion. I've yet to write the definitive biography and…I want to be a cowboy."

She slowly shook her head. "What is wrong with you, Nick?"

"The list I gave you isn't enough?"

"No, I mean what's brought this on? I've never seen you like this."

"Do you know much about Frank Truman?" he asked.

She shrugged. "Not really. He wasn't a cowboy, though, was he?"

"Not literally. But he was the type. Big, swaggering. Take-no-prisoners sort of chap."

"And you want to be like that?"

"Would you find it attractive?"

"No. I don't think I would."

"Really?" Nick felt his spirits lift slightly. "But don't women secretly want that macho swagger stuff?"

"Don't men secretly want air-headed bits of fluff?"

"Yes, they do."

Gillian hit his arm. "No, they don't. Not *all* men." The waitress delivered their drinks. Gillian sipped hers, then set it carefully down on the paper coaster. "I could be wrong," she said, "and you don't have to tell me if you don't want to, but I have this feeling…call it intuition." She met Nick's eyes across the table. "You've met someone, haven't you?"

HE COULDN'T SLEEP. The illuminated seconds, minutes and hours blinked inexorably away on his bedside clock, and he lay in bed wide awake, despite yawning his head off earlier in the evening. He couldn't sleep, and he couldn't rouse himself sufficiently to get up and start work. The dog, who had not demolished the sofa cushions, was asleep at the foot of the bed. He watched it for a moment. In the dim light, it didn't seem quite as ugly as he'd first thought—although the proportions were definitely off.

He wondered if Daisy would find it ugly when she saw it tomorrow. Probably not. In Daisy's eyes, he imagined, there was no such thing as an ugly animal. Hands pillowed behind his head, he pictured her as she'd looked that afternoon. When she'd walked into the restaurant, she'd been wearing a wide-brimmed straw hat, her long, reddish-brown curls escaping over one shoulder.

She wasn't beautiful—he could imagine Valerie making tart observations about her size. Healthy, in his opinion. Valerie would probably say plump. There was an earthy, natural quality about her that he found appealing, though. If he'd answered Gillian's question honestly, he would have confessed that he'd been blindsided by Daisy Fowler.

"One minute, I'm congratulating myself on finally managing a face-to-face meeting with her…" he would have said "…the next I'm pouring my heart out—or if not my heart, my parental frustrations. Looking back, I honestly can't say how it happened."

Daisy had been telling him about some volunteer work she did at a Children's Hospital, he recalled now, and he'd been stoking the damn fire. Wildfires burning all over the state—ninety-degree heat, and there he'd been in a restaurant kitchen, stoking a bloody great fireplace.

"…I just go and hold the babies," she'd said. "The mothers, some of them, don't visit. They're on drugs, and sometimes they don't even remember they've had a kid."

She'd been chopping the scarlet peppers that Toby later knocked to the floor, her head bent, focused on the task. "Babies just tear me up," she'd said. "All babies, even those whose mothers aren't all messed up. You look into those big, innocent eyes and, really, how could you not feel good about the human race? The baby smiles and you can't help it—you just have to smile back. Maybe if everybody could look at each other and just see that basic baby goodness, it would make life a whole lot easier."

With this thought in mind, Nick finally drifted off to sleep.

DAISY SAT IN the bleachers of the Laguna Tennis Club, watching Emily, in pigtails and baggy shorts, lose—again—to a blonde in white Lycra who was seeded eighth in the tournament and who probably outweighed Emily—who was not seeded—by about fifteen pounds. Daisy had never seen the other girl, but she had visions of herself leaping like Super-woman over the bleachers and onto the court, grabbing Emmy's tennis racket and braining her sleek, golden head.

To hell with sportsmanship, she was a mother. Although, to be perfectly honest, there were a few less than thrilling moments when Emmy batted the ball back and forth with no discernable enthusiasm that Daisy felt her attention wander. The thought of seeing Nick again in a few hours was a tempting distraction, although she did have to keep reminding herself that it was just to hand off the dog.

Another reason her mind wasn't completely on the game was last night's dream about her father. Not the candle flame one this time, just a jumble of images, but now she couldn't get him out of her head.

Emmy took after her grandfather. That morning, still in the bedroom getting dressed, she'd heard Emmy talking on the phone in the kitchen. Something hushed and secretive about her daughter's voice had made her think of her father's whispered phone conversations and the way he'd stop talking and make some obvious excuse to the caller when he realized he was no longer alone.

"Good job," she called as Emily returned a shot with a surprisingly energetic backhand that sent her opponent scurrying across the court. The rally was brief, though, and thoughts of her father reclaimed Daisy's attention.

He'd been secretive for reasons she hadn't really understood then and didn't now. Hoarding things, squirrel-like, and protective of any encroachment upon his personal space. A Portuguese house-keeper—a distant relative of Amalia's—had briefly tried to instill order in their lives until she had inadvertently thrown away his collection of toilet paper from fourteen countries. He'd sacked her on the spot.

But the housekeeper had contributed a word to their vocabulary. *Lixo.* It meant rubbish and in her view described pretty much everything in the house—the assortment of wineglasses with broken stems, plastic sunglasses sans lenses, twigs and bits of wood, metal from a building site, rocks, pebbles from their beachcombing expeditions, chunks of mosaic paving stone—all piled onto any and every available surface.

The house had been huge. Six bedrooms, a massive living room and meandering passageways, but it was absolutely filled with her father's *lixo.* One time he'd arranged for a helicopter to lift a huge granite rock off a beach in Scotland, then had had it shipped to California, where he'd installed it in Daisy's bedroom, the only room in the house not filled to capacity. Objects brought from other places, he'd tell her, even a stone off the beach, carried the spirit of that place. Their house had been an international spirit bazaar.

Mostly, though, he'd use the *lixo* to make sculptures, sometimes enlisting her help in the creation.

They might spend hours assembling a piece. Or two or three weeks, even months. No one but the two of them ever saw the finished pieces. "They're our creations, Daisy," he would say. "Reveal them to the world's eyes and they become diminished. People come up with their idiotic interpretations and the spirit is destroyed."

As a young child, she'd been enchanted with his whimsy. In her teens, she'd grown embarrassed by it all. "Dad…" she'd complain when they could no longer sit at the dining room table because it was stacked almost to the ceiling with his *lixo* "…can't we get rid of some of this?" But, of course, she knew the answer.

They never had another housekeeper. Housework, such as it was, fell largely to her. Ironically, her father complained constantly that she didn't keep the place clean. "Filthy," he'd pronounce, running his finger in the dusty grease on the hood of the stove. "I can't live with filth." He'd resolved the problem, finally, by just cleaning his half of everything: his half of the stove where he cooked his egg and bacon for breakfast every morning; his half of the kitchen counter where he buttered his toast; his half, or the part that wasn't cluttered with *lixo,* of the giant mahogany bureau in the entry hall.

"Dad." she'd once screamed at him in frustration after coming home to find his half of the stove immaculately clean while her half was splattered in spaghetti sauce. "My half was clean when I left. *You* cooked the spaghetti on *my* half. I wasn't here. How could I have cleaned it?

"I clean my half," he'd said. "I'm satisfied with the arrangement."

Or the time he'd ranted about cobwebs. Yet she'd come home to find him laughing to himself as he decorated them with dead flies, old eyeglasses, even a snapshot of herself as a baby.

Life with her father had been that way for as long as she could remember. She'd never even given it much thought. It was just the way he was.

"Ever occur to you that Emmy is embarrassed by you and your hippy friends?"

Daisy shook her head, she didn't want to think.

Heat shimmered up in waves from the court where Emmy was clearly resigned to losing. Daisy's heart ached as she watched her daughter drag herself around the court as though her shoes were filled with lead. Last year if this had happened, she would have been able to fix it with hugs and pep talks and root beer floats. But now, as she watched her little girl— who wore a bra and had started shaving her legs, despite Daisy's protests that the soft, blond fuzz would return as coarse, dark hair—she wondered if her maternal instincts, which had always seemed infallible, were now failing her.

On the court, Emmy's opponent delivered the final blow, winning the match in easy victory. After both girls had shaken hands and left the court, Daisy started to get up, but someone pulled her back down. Toby.

"Thought I'd catch the game," he said.

"One, you've missed it," she said without looking at him. "And two, I'd rather not talk to you right now. After your tantrum yesterday, I'm not sure I really want to talk to you again, period."

"I'm sorry," he said, finally. "I was right in the middle of planning dinner, and you kind of threw me when you ordered me out."

"I didn't order you out," Daisy said, although she supposed he was right in a way. Here we go again, she thought. My fault as usual. "I didn't appreciate the way you acted."

"I'm sorry, okay?" He folded his arms. "So. You decided to talk to Nick after all, huh? You guys looked pretty cozy when I got back."

"He was telling me about his daughter," Daisy said, sounding defensive to her own ears and wondering why she even needed to offer an explanation.

"Yeah, well, if he's such a hot-shot father, what's he doing over here when his kid's back in England?"

The sun was blazing right down on them, searing the top of her head, and the wind had picked up, heating the air to low-oven temperatures. Daisy turned in her seat to look at Toby. Beneath the brim of his baseball hat, embroidered with the Wildfire logo, his face was flushed and he was perspiring

"What exactly is your problem?" she asked. "You want to tell me what's *really* bothering you?"

"You can leave, now Toby," he said in a mincing voice. "You don't tell me when to leave. Maybe I don't have some fancy accent and go jetting off writing books, but I was good enough for you when your father was going crazy and you didn't have anyone else to run to, so just remember that, okay?"

Daisy didn't answer. Toby had obviously made Nick into his "bear," reacting jealously to what he perceived as something going on between her and Nick, which was ridiculous. Well, wasn't it?

"...and if you think Mr. Fancy Biographer's really interested in your damn animals and all your sob stories, you're nuts. Just don't say I didn't warn you."

And then he was gone. At the foot of the bleachers, Daisy saw Emmy wave. Adrenaline still pumping, she forced a calm, friendly expression and went down to meet her daughter.

"Hey, sweetie." She peered into Emmy's face, still pink from heat and exertion. "How you feeling?"

"Fine," Emmy said sullenly.

"You played a good game," she said.

"No, I didn't." Emmy's voice was indignant. "Did you even watch it? I sucked, big time."

"But you gave it your best." Daisy wasn't entirely sure this was true, but she didn't care. She wished her father had said this to her just once, she'd have been ecstatic. "That's what counts. Hey, come on…wanna go with me to pick up a puppy?"

"A puppy?" Emmy's surliness faded. "Where?"

"This guy Nick…the biographer. He rescued one and he can't keep it."

"Nick?"

"Right."

"Dad said he's…" She scuffed her tennis shoe on the wooden bleacher. "Forget it."

Daisy blew air out through her mouth. Toby was walking a very fine line these days. "So you want to come with me or not?

"What's the puppy like?"

"I don't know, I haven't seen it. Ugly, Nick said."

Emily rolled her eyes. "Like we need another dog."

"Emily?" When her animal-loving daughter failed to get excited over a puppy, *something* was wrong, and instinct told her it was more than just losing the game. Daisy tipped her finger under her daughter's chin. "Honey?"

"I'm fine." She swatted Daisy's hand away. "Quit making such a big deal about everything." She scuffed her sneaker at the wooden step. "Dad's here. I'm going surfing with him."

CHAPTER TEN

DAISY HAD SAID SHE'D call after her daughter's tennis match.

Nick glanced at the clock in the right-hand corner of the laptop's screen: 2:00 p.m. Had he asked her what time the match ended? Had he asked her daughter's name?

Had he called his own daughter?

He set the laptop on the small balcony table, walked inside and dialed Bella's number. No answer. It would be…almost eight in the evening in London. What would a twelve-year-old child be doing at almost eight in the evening? Shouldn't she be home in bed? Why didn't he know the answer to either of these questions? He hung up without leaving a message.

Back on the balcony, he tried to organize his notes on Truman. The sun was shining on the screen, making it difficult to read anything, but it didn't really matter because he'd made very little progress in the past two days. And he already knew, having actually met Daisy Fowler, that she would be less help than hindrance.

He should have clarified whether she'd meant to call him immediately after the match. If he knew where the tennis courts were, he could just drive over and meet her. Drop the dog off and get back to work. Speaking of the dog. It had wriggled half its body through the bars of the railings and was yapping at a squirrel on the shrub-covered slope. He retrieved the dog and carried it back into the apartment just in case the manager happened to walk by. Earlier, he'd walked over to the coffee house for his morning dose and, on the way back, had noticed a pet shop. Half an hour and fifty dollars later, he'd walked out with a padded basket, some biscuits and a toy shaped like a hot dog. He'd told himself he hadn't bought the stuff to impress Daisy, but he wasn't quite sure he believed it.

He set the dog in the basket, whereupon it immediately climbed out and peed on the carpet. Nick regarded it for a moment. Knobby, misshapen head, tail like a ratty feather duster; ridiculously long nose and massive meat plates for feet. "You are ugly," he said. "Moreover, you're straining my patience."

The dog looked up at him in much the way he might look at Cameron Diaz. Misty-eyed, drooling, tongue hanging out. "I am not, even remotely, growing fond of you," Nick said.

The phone rang.

"Dude."

"Sorry?"

"Toby Fowler. What's happening?"

Nick dropped into the armchair. He decided not to mention Daisy's imminent visit. "Work, for the most part. How about yourself?"

"I got my daughter with me right now. Gonna give her a surf lesson." His voice lowered. "Hey, you wanna meet some really hot chicks, I mean like major hot?"

Nick laughed. He couldn't help himself. He stuck his feet up on the coffee table, tipped his head back. "Women you personally know, Toby?" he asked politely.

"Hey, Laguna's a small town, I know everyone. Seriously. Chicks in bikinis all over the place. Grab your stuff and come on down here, I'll teach you to surf."

"Thanks, but I'll have to take you up some other time. Work…"

"Yeah… So, anyway, you and Daisy, like, got to talk yesterday?"

"Yes, we did." Nick suspected they'd arrived at the reason for the call. "Thanks for your, uh, assistance."

"No *problemo*," Toby said. "She give you anything good?"

It took him a moment to work out what Toby meant. And the answer, really, was no, but he didn't intend to report back on his conversations to Toby or anyone else. "Everything's useful to some extent."

"Yeah, well…just remember what I told you about Daisy. She can be real naïve at times, that's why *I'm* still around. We've got a daughter together, someone needs to look out for both of them. Make sure nobody screws with them, if you know what I mean."

"Right," Nick said. He'd been warned. After Toby said goodbye, Nick got a beer from the fridge and was just about to open it when the phone rang again. This time it was Daisy.

"I'm out on the boardwalk," she said. "Probably right outside your apartment. It's the big gray building with balconies over the ocean and the white umbrellas on the roof?"

"Hold on." Smiling, he carried the phone out to the balcony. "Definitely ocean-facing and—" he glanced up "—yes white umbrellas up on the sun deck." He leaned over the edge of the balcony and peered down the boardwalk. He could see Daisy, red hair blowing about her face, wearing a denim jacket and white cotton trousers. She was looking up at the building. And when she saw him she waved. "The other identifying feature is a good-looking chap with a phone in his hand," he said.

"Good-looking chap? Hmm…"

"Look harder."

"Oh yeah, I think I see him. What about the dog?"

"Dog's right here." Nick glanced at his feet. "Licking my toes."

"I'll be right up."

"Wait where you are, I'll bring him down." He hung up, grabbed the dog, started down the stairs, remembered the pee on the carpet, ran back up, sponged it clean, then made his way down again. "*Phew.*"

Daisy, waiting with her arms folded across her chest, smiled and held out her arms for the dog. Nick handed it over and watched it go into an orgy of face-licking, tail-wagging, whimpering delirium in Daisy's arms. *Lucky stiff.*

"It's not ugly," Daisy said, holding the dog at arm's length to see its face. "It has character and it's a—" She peered at its belly "—a he. Perfect, he'll get along with the girls. And the new girl that was just dropped by the other day."

"How many do you have?" Nick asked, without taking his eyes off her and the dog, half-buried now in Daisy's long hair.

"Four…five. Come here, you." She maneuvered the dog off her shoulder, held it in her arms like a baby. "Who's a sweet boy?"

"I suppose we…you should come up with a name for it, him," Nick said, already wondering, now that he'd handed the dog over, what excuse he could come up with to keep Daisy around for a while. "Any ideas?"

"I thought I'd let Emmy name him."

"Good idea." Inspiration struck. "Would you like to take him for a walk?"

"You mean me?" She looked amused. "Or are you inviting yourself along?"

"If you'd like to have me," he said, politely.

"Sure." Daisy grinned at him. "We need a leash, though. That's how he got into trouble the first time."

"There's a pet shop across the road."

TOBY STOOD at the entrance to the movie theater, where he could duck behind the ticket booth if Daisy or Mr. Fancy Schmancy happened to look across the road. Fat chance. They were standing on the boardwalk by Main Beach—where he'd wanted to go check out the babes in bikinis, except Emily decided she needed to go look at makeup instead. And that was how he happened to be in the right place to see Daisy and Nick. Emmy had gone into the drugstore to spend the ten bucks he'd given her that was burning a hole in her pocket, and he'd gone around the back of the place to smoke a joint. Okay, okay, he wasn't going to do it anymore especially when Emily might smell it on his clothes, but he was so mad at Daisy, the way she was talking to him like he was nothing, he needed to do *something*.

And there's Daisy holding the damn dog, and the biographer's practically drooling, just like the dog. Jeez, he could hardly watch. Her hand on his arm, head to one side like, "Oh, I'm such a girly girl how can you resist me?" She had her back to the ocean and the winds were whipping everything—the waves, her hair, the ends of her shirt. The biographer's jacket.

It didn't take a brain surgeon to figure out that Daisy already had the hots for the guy. He heard Emmy call him and took one last look. Daisy had it coming, that's all he had to say.

THEY WALKED AND WALKED for hours until finally Daisy decided that the puppy had had enough, and they took turns carrying it.

"The problem with living here my whole life," she said, "is that I don't really see it any more. Like driving the truck down Pacific Coast Highway. Instead of admiring the way the coastline curves, I'm cursing the traffic and calculating how long it will take to get to the market. Or I'm looking up at the hills and all I see is that one more Craftsman Cottage has given way to some gaudy McMansion."

Nick nodded, offering an example of his own about living in London, cursing the traffic around Trafalgar Square because of all the damn tourists snapping pictures with the pigeons. The thought of actual work had barely crossed his mind.

"My father never stopped *seeing* Laguna," Daisy said. "To the point that he couldn't see that traffic was threatening to choke the two roads leading out of town, or that all the development was threatening the delicate ecological balance. I guess he was in denial. You know, you see what you want to see."

Nick filed this away. Daisy had carefully handed over the dog as she was talking, a move that caused her long hair to fall briefly over his face. He'd smelled the light, clean tang of her shampoo. While he might have read the scrap of information about her father as a sign she was opening up, might have felt it appropriate to introduce a question or two, instead he'd shifted the sleeping dog to a more comfortable position and they'd just kept walking.

Daisy told him about Laguna's secret stairways just south of town that only locals knew about, flights of steps leading down to the beach. "They're kind of hidden between big fancy houses, and most of them don't have signs or anything," she explained. "If you're driving, you have to find somewhere to park on PCH, which is always a hassle. Once you start walking down the stairs, though, you forget all the traffic on the highway."

Because they were both on foot, parking wasn't a problem, and, since he wanted nothing more than to prolong this walk with Daisy, he suggested they visit one of the stairways. By the time they reached the first flight, the sun was beginning its nightly melt into the Pacific.

They stood at the top of the stairs, a steep, vertical drop of three hundred feet or so down to the sea.

Daisy glanced at him, smiled slightly and, without a word, they started walking down, past stands of lush vegetation and picture-postcard views of the Pacific edged by miles of pristine white sand, tinted pink by the setting sun. The sun had also colored the windows of the clifftop mansions a blazing vermillion, burnishing the air with a rosy glow. It was as though, Nick remarked to Daisy, someone had just yelled, "Special lighting needed," and flipped a switch.

At the foot of the stairs, they craned their necks to look back up.

It took him a moment to convince himself that the house he was looking at wasn't on fire. When he turned back to face the ocean again, the water and the sky were the color of tangerines. Daisy watched him, smiling.

"It's like a performance," he said.

"People line up along the cliffs to watch," she said, as the giant orange orb slowly melted on the horizon. "They even bring deckchairs. And when it's all over, they applaud."

A few minutes later, they climbed back up the steps, the light still suffused with pink and orange. And then, just as though a light had gone out, the show was over.

"I'm starving," Daisy said.

THEY ENDED UP at the Beach Shack, a dimly lit deli off Pacific Coast Highway.

One of the last remnants of the old Laguna Beach, Daisy told Nick and the only place in town that wouldn't make a big deal about the dog.

"The Laguna Beach of longhairs and a holistic lifestyle," she said. "My father's generation, except he wasn't exactly holistic."

As he glanced up at the pastel-colored chalkboard menus that loomed over their heads, Nick felt vaguely disconcerted. Another hint that it was all right to start asking questions? He decided against it. Caution was still the operative word, and, for the time being, Truman was just Daisy's father and the definitive biography seemed about as distant as the setting sun.

"The breakfast burritos are yummy," Daisy said.

"Breakfast?" He was reading the other offerings. Breakfast was evidently a big deal. Granola was listed as a special; served all day.

"What on earth is a fusion pita?" he asked, pointing to an item scribbled in yellow chalk.

"It's a sandwich filled with whatever you want…grilled eggplant tabbouleh, feta cheese and red peppers. Good roughage. "

Nick laughed. "That's always a concern."

"Tell you what, I'll order and you go find somewhere to sit." Daisy pointed to a row of wooden trestle tables under a bamboo canopy partially covered with foliage.

He found a spot and in a short time they were unwrapping wax paper from sandwiches the size and shape of small torpedoes. Daisy reeled off the contents, many things he'd never even heard of. The one thing he would have recognized, he couldn't find. "Where's the cheese?"

"Look inside," Daisy said. "It's probably there."

He investigated, found it melted onto the pita, thin as a coating of butter, trapping wisps of bean sprouts and bits of cucumber. "What's that?" He pointed at Daisy's bowl, filled with something that looked like yellow rice.

"Tabbouleh."

"I thought tabbouleh was green."

"Different ingredients." She poked around with the plastic fork. "Some squash there, I think. Here." She held out her fork for him to taste.

"Good." He smiled. Everything was good. He felt suffused with a sudden and almost giddy happiness. They shared a bag of tortilla chips, locally made, Daisy said, sipped at drinks made with fruit and yogurt.

"Nick…" Daisy had pulled a long piece of grilled eggplant from her sandwich and was holding it between her thumb and forefinger as though deciding whether or not to eat it. "What's the story on your daughter's mother?"

The question jolted him out of a vaguely dream-like state. One minute they were in a funky Laguna dive and he was feeling vaguely remiss about his complete lack of interest in her father, the next she was catapulting them back to London, his daughter and a time in his life he preferred not to think about. He eyed the greenish-yellow liquid oozing from his pita. "We're divorced,' he said. Daisy kept looking at him. "Avril was pregnant when we got married."

"You were the father?"

"Right. At the time, I was supporting myself with freelance writing—I hadn't discovered biographies—and my income was precarious at best. She wanted to get married. I didn't."

Head bowed, Daisy kept poking around at her food with a plastic fork. "Couldn't find the peppers," she said. "Now I have." She looked up at him. "Very supportive of you, huh?"

Nick set down his sandwich. "We *did* get married though and she *did* have the baby."

Daisy smiled, but said nothing.

He drank some of the yogurt concoction. "If I sound defensive—"

"You do. How come?"

He started to answer, then stopped. "I have a new name for you. Daisy the Interrogator."

She laughed. "I know, it's a bad habit of mine. Sorry, I don't mean to give you a hard time. I had such a…how should I describe it? An unconventional childhood that I'm just curious about how other people raise their kids."

Nick reminded himself of why he was in Laguna. "Tell me more," he wanted to say. "It's not easy, being a parent," he said instead.

Daisy grinned. "You've got that right."

"Do you and Toby share custody of your daughter?"

"I have custody. He has visitation rights."

"Toby's…an interesting character."

She rolled her eyes. "That's one way of putting it."

"I was wondering——

"Why I put up with him?"

Nick nodded.

"Because…" She bit her lip. "Hmm. Uh, this is almost harder to talk about than my father—"

"Don't if you'd rather not.'

"It's okay. Sometimes carrying all this stuff around is…I knew Toby in high school, but he wasn't a close friend. I didn't really have any close friends— my dad took up all my time. But when my dad started getting difficult, I began hanging out at this place down in Dana Point where Toby worked. He was the bartender. So I'd unload all the stuff about my dad, and we just got closer and soon he was the only person I could really talk to. And then…well, we did more than talk and I got pregnant…"

Nick waited. After the brief eye contact, she'd looked away. Hadn't looked at him once since. Now she was dissecting her food again: strips of red pepper, more eggplant, a sodden slice of cucumber. He took a bite of his sandwich, set it down.

"I thought my life was over," she said. "I was supposed to be going to college and just the thought of telling my dad…"

Her voice trailed off. He waited.

"Anyway, Toby talked me out of an abortion."

"Toby talked you out of it?"

"Yeah." She gave a wry smile. "Surprising, huh? You'd think it would be the other way around."

"Did he want to marry you?"

"Absolutely. He was like a salesman. He'd paint these rosy pictures of this great life we'd have together. But I didn't love him…well, I did as a friend, he was very sweet and supportive. So we got married…but we didn't live happily ever after."

"His hold on you is your daughter, then?"

"Pretty much. I look at Emmy sometimes and the guilt over how much I wanted the abortion can literally make me cry." A faint smile flickered across her face. "See? Even talking about it does a number on me. Emmy doesn't know the whole story and I'd do almost anything for her not to know it."

"Including putting up with Toby?"

"Including putting up with Toby."

"He threatens to tell her?"

She nodded.

"Maybe it would be better for her to know the truth."

"Does *your* daughter know the truth?"

Nick put his elbows on the table, held his head in his hands and stared at her. "I honestly don't know what her mother's told her. If Bella knows, she's never mentioned it to me."

Daisy shook her head reprovingly. "Nick." And then her expression lightened. "Uh-oh. Here I go again…any time you need to feel like a total jerk, just call."

"No disrespect to your talent, but I frequently manage that without any assistance." He sat back a little. The place had emptied out, a kid in jeans and a UCLA T-shirt was sweeping the floor. "Bella wants very much to come out here."

"So why doesn't she?"

"Well, she's still in school for starters." He met her eyes. "And I'm here to work."

Daisy got very involved in picking vegetables out of her sandwich. "Love these red peppers."

Nick nodded. He was starting to feel disoriented. One minute Daisy was a woman he found incredibly appealing and attractive, the next she was the difference between the success or failure of the work he was in Laguna to do.

Suddenly, without giving it a thought, he reached across the table and circled her wrist. The move surprised him as much as it obviously had Daisy. They both looked down. Daisy's wrist was small and freckled, fragile as a bird. The cuff of her denim jacket brushed the back of his hand.

"Daisy," he said.

She smiled. "That's me."

And then her smile faded and the silence lengthened. Two vertical lines appeared on her forehead. "This is like the elephant in the living room," she finally said. "I've been putting it off and putting it off, but…Nick, this biography. I mean you seem like a really nice guy and everything, but I think it would be better if we just dropped it."

He was still holding her wrist. She pulled away.

"Mostly I'm concerned about Amalia, my stepmother. She's kind of fragile emotionally. My dad was the love of her life, and it devastated her when he died."

Nick said nothing.

"She's never really recovered from Dad's death," Daisy said. "She has her good days, but there are others where…" She shook her head. "It's like stirring a tide pool. The water looks clear and calm, but then things start coming to the surface."

"Sometimes that can be a good thing," he said. "Things fester in the dark, sometimes it's better to let in a little fresh air."

She looked at him so intently that he thought for a moment he'd persuaded her. Then she slowly shook her head. "I'm sorry," she said.

CHAPTER ELEVEN

"PERFECT FIRE WEATHER," the white-haired gallery owner in the Hawaiian shirt observed the following morning over breakfast at the Jolly Roger restaurant. "Drought conditions, ninety-degree heat, three percent humidity and an eighty-five mile-per-hour Santa Ana wind. And, for good measure, a bumper crop of combustible wood-frame houses." He grinned across the table at Nick. "The price you pay for living in paradise, eh?"

"Beats London in November," Nick said, leaning back to let the waitress refill his coffee cup. It was the stock answer he often gave, but suddenly he was having doubts. The fires were always burning somewhere. The nightly TV news' pictures of people rescuing animals from blazing hillsides, or hosing down rooftops, the ash in the air, all combined to give him the disgruntled sense that the price for living in paradise might be higher than he personally would want to pay.

And he was back to square one on the biography.

He would call Martin today, he'd decided, but he had an intuitive sense that Daisy had made up her mind. He'd give it a day or so, then ring her. Inquire about the dog, perhaps. He returned his attention to his breakfast companion.

Max Bowen owned one of the larger art galleries in Laguna, an oceanfront studio with a panoramic view of coastline that competed with the high-priced painted depictions for sale on the walls. A self-described dabbler himself, Max, a fit-looking seventy-five-year-old, had been a friend of Frank Truman, whose work had also hung in Bowen's gallery.

"So how do you like Laguna so far?" Max asked as he mopped up egg yolk with a rolled up tortilla.

Nick smiled. "Very nice."

"You've come at a good time. Summer, you can't move for tourists. Pacific Coast Highway—" He waved his tortilla at the winding thoroughfare behind Nick, one of only two roads in and out of town. "It's not the place it used to be, though. Fifty years back, when I first came here, it really was an artists' colony. Now it's mostly tourists and millionaires building bigger and bigger places that either burn down or fall down. You've heard about the fires burning up north?"

Nick nodded. Last night had been cool and foggy, but this morning, when he'd gone across the road to pick up the newspaper, the air had already been warm and smelled faintly of smoke.

Max ate for a few minutes in silence, using a tortilla to heap beans onto his fork. "How's the book going?"

"Not bad." He drank some coffee. "I'm particularly interested in how Frank's relationship with his daughter influenced his work as an artist." He described the experience of seeing Truman's painting for the first time. "My sense is that the magical quality of the painting was largely a reflection of Truman's feelings for Daisy." He glanced down at the notebook he'd set on the table, looked up at Max. "Quite frankly, as the father of a young daughter, I was envious. Of Truman's artistic ability but also of the life I imagined they must have led."

Max gave him a long look. "Yeah, well, Frank changed after Daisy was born. Before that, he was quite the skirt-chaser. That's why Amalia left him that first time, that and she was a whacky broad anyway."

"How exactly?"

"Well, she drank. Drinks. Is she out of the hospital?"

"I believe so."

"Have you met her yet?"

"Not so far." She hadn't answered his messages, and he wondered if she and Daisy had reached a mutual agreement on the biography.

"You've heard the talk, I guess?"

"About?"

"You know Frank died in a house fire, right? Fifty

other houses burned down that night, but Frank was the only fatality. Didn't take long for the rumors to start."

Nick waited.

"One theory went that he didn't really die in the fire, he just wanted to get away from Amalia. The other is that he did, but the fire was set by someone who had something to cover up. Conspiracy theories, you know the kind of thing. Amalia was drinking too much, Daisy was giving him trouble."

"Daisy? In what way?"

Max grinned. "You got teenagers? That's what they do, give their folks grief. Daisy was no better or worse, but she was down in the village, hanging out with other kids, the way teenagers do. And then she takes up with this local boy, Toby, and I guess that's when she and Frank started clashing. You met Toby?"

"Yes, I have." He felt Max waiting for him to say more, but decided against any personal observations.

"Only reason he has a restaurant is Daisy's money. Frank left everything to her. I'm not saying he doesn't do a good job, they say he's a pretty damn good chef, but…I dunno, I never cared for the kid. He's not exactly a kid anymore, I guess, gotta be mid-forties. But at my age, anything under fifty's a kid. Toby, he's a smooth talker, always got his eye on the money, it seems to me."

Nick remained diplomatically silent.

"They've got a kid together. Cute little girl.

Daddy's girl, from what I've seen. Spends a lot of time with Toby, probably why Daisy puts up with him. Anyway, the old man wasn't happy about Toby. So one school of thought is they got into a fight—"

"Daisy and her father?"

"Right, and things escalated and she shot him."

"Shot him?" Nick tried not to gape. "Seems like a stretch, doesn't it? Why would anyone think that?"

"Frank was a big gun collector. Used to take Daisy on hunting trips. She certainly knew how to use a gun. The other scenario is that Toby killed the old man. He married Daisy a few months after Frank died."

"So you're saying what? That the fire was deliberately set to cover up the murder?"

"I'm not saying that's what happened." Max motioned for the waitress. "I'm just telling you about the rumors that were going around after Frank died. And the thing with the fire, well, fires were burning all over Orange County that night. Most of Laguna had been evacuated. The winds were erratic, jumping all over the place. Frank's house could have been burned down by one of the wildfires, or someone could have just struck a match."

Nick massaged the back of his neck. He'd anticipated a discussion of Truman's art. This murder theory made his head spin. *My brother has detractors, Martin Truman had said.*

Max grinned. "You look sucker-punched."

"It's bit of a shocker," Nick said. "But, you mentioned Amalia…"

"Amalia." He shook his head. "I told you, Amalia's kind of a headcase, but she was always nuts about Frank. If she'd set the fire, she'd have made sure she burned up in it with him."

"POOR DEANNA," the parrot said. "Poor Deanna's a pretty girl."

"No, you're not," Daisy muttered from the fridge, where she was checking out possible comfort food. "You're ugly and green, and your feathers are falling out."

Nothing remotely appealing. She closed the fridge door, wandered into the bathroom and took off all her clothes. If she was down a pound, or even at the same weight, she'd bake a Wacky cake. Emmy liked Wacky cake.

She closed her eyes, bracing herself for the bad news that would reveal itself in two-inch-high green digits. She'd bought the scale two months ago after deciding, once and for all, to get serious about losing weight. This scale replaced the old one with its black lines marking quarter pounds. If she didn't wear her glasses when she stepped on the scale—and of course she didn't because every ounce counted—the little black lines all blurred together, making it too easy to fudge, no pun intended.

But the new scale, with the cat's-eye-green digital readout, was merciless, flashing the verdict like an electronic gossip. Today's big news? Up half a pound.

How could that be?

Damn, damn, double-damn.

She'd actually been losing weight until Nick came to town. Last night had just made things a whole lot worse. Saying no to the biographer had been one thing. Saying no to Nick was something else. She went into the kitchen, where, before she realized what she was doing, she'd assembled all the ingredients for a Wacky cake.

Things fester in the dark, Nick had said last night. *Sometimes it's better to let in a little fresh air.*

She beat sugar, cocoa and flour together. How different would things have been, she sometimes wondered, if she'd had a mother in her life? Not that Amalia wasn't wonderful and dear, but would her father's impact on her have been less profound if, instead of taking everything he said and did to heart, she'd had someone to casually dismiss his more cutting remarks. "Oh, don't take any notice, honey. You know how your father is."

She'd woken twisted in her sheets, her hair damp with sweat. The candle dream again. Yesterday, on the beach with Nick, they'd looked up and seen the sun reflected in the windows of the house on the cliff. He'd thought the house was on fire. People always did. It was an old trick her father had played on visitors to town. "Quick," he'd say. "Call the fire department. There's a phone booth up there at the top of the stairs." And he'd laugh uproariously, not letting them in on the joke until they'd climbed at least half of the stairs.

Would Nick have thought that funny? If he'd written the biography, would he have interpreted it in some way that made her father look…what? Nuts? Really, how could Nick, who had never met her father, interpret the stories she told him when she didn't know what to make of them herself?

In the two or three years before he had died, he had seemed to her like two different men. Thinking about him, she'd literally *see* two different men in her mind. For as long as she could remember, he'd worn a mustache. It was gray and bristly and it tickled her cheek when he hugged her. And then one day he'd shaved it off. He hadn't said anything, just walked into the living room where she'd been lying on the couch reading a book and casually asked what she was reading.

For a moment, all she'd noticed was that he looked different somehow and then she'd seen the mustache was gone. He'd grinned, waiting for her reaction.

She'd blurted out the first thought that came to her. "You have no upper lip." It was true, she could see his face now. In profile, the absence of an upper lip made him looked carved somehow, like one of those faces on a totem pole. An easy face to carve: one smooth straight line from nose to chin, broken only by a slit for the mouth, no fuss over the curve of lips. With his mouth exposed, he looked stern and unyielding. The mustache had hidden something mean, it had seemed to her, which was now revealed.

He hadn't spoken to her for the rest of the night and now, when she looked back on her father as two different men, it all seemed to start with the mustache.

Good Dad had a mustache and he'd laugh and sing and think up fun stuff to do. Sometimes he'd get angry over trivial things and people's stupidity—everyone in the world was stupid except him and possibly her, although she hadn't his brilliance or she'd be doing something with her life instead of hanging around Laguna coffeeshops with deadbeat surfers.

Bad Dad never physically abused her, never did horrible things to her, it was just this steady drip, drip, drip of childish, vindictive venom. She'd watch him in his Bad Dad moods, study his profile—flattish forehead, the jut of nose, a lipless slit of a mouth and an ordinary-looking chin. Usually a pulse twitched in his cheek. *What did I do?* she'd wonder, reviewing the day's mundane events. *What did I do?*

Life hadn't met his expectations and she knew, deep down inside, that in some way he'd never articulated to her, she was responsible for turning Good Dad to Bad Dad.

"Hey, Mom." Emmy appeared in the kitchen. "What are you doing?"

"Making Wacky cake."

"Are you stressed or something?"

"I thought you liked it."

"I hate it. You always make it when you're in a bad mood. If I smell it in the oven, I stay away."

Daisy laughed. "You do not."

Outside, the dogs started barking excitedly and when she went to the window, she saw two of the bigger ones circling the puppy. He was clearly holding his own, yapping and dancing in circles, his ungainly body comically endearing.

"That's the puppy?" Emmy asked.

"Yep. We…Nick and I took him for a long walk."

"I thought you didn't want to talk to him."

"I don't particularly want to talk to him about Granddad, but he's kind of interesting to talk to about other things."

"So was it like, a date?"

"No, it wasn't *like* a date. It wasn't a date, period." Not that she'd had any thoughts that it might be— except maybe the moment when Nick had caught her wrist. But if she had, Nick's cool formality after she'd told him the biography was off erased any doubts.

"I got back here just before you did," she said, in case Emmy had some idea that she'd been out half the night. In fact, she'd been in the bedroom looking for a book to read when she'd heard Emmy come in. As she'd started to call out, she'd heard Toby's voice in the living room and decided she wasn't in the mood to deal with him. Toby had stayed for a while, probably figuring she'd eventually come out, but she'd drifted off to sleep. When she'd wakened around midnight, Emmy was in bed asleep.

"So, what else d'you do?"

Daisy put the cake in the oven. Emily was sitting at the kitchen table, her arms crossed. The inquisitorial tone in her voice reminded Daisy of the way she'd grilled Nick. *Daisy the Interrogator*. And after all that, she'd told him no on the book.

"Earth to Mom," Emmy said.

"I told you." Daisy looked at her daughter. "We went for a long walk, down those steps by Monarch Bay, along the beach. Then we had dinner at the Beach Shack."

Emmy made a face. She didn't like the food there.

"So, what kind of car does he have?"

"Car?" Daisy shook her head. "I've no idea. Why?"

"Dad said he has a ton of money."

"Nick? He said Nick had a ton of money?" How exactly would Toby know that? And why was Toby discussing Nick with Emmy, anyway? It seemed so odd to think that Toby would actually be jealous of Nick, as though there was anything really to be jealous of. And yet…sitting across from him at the Beach Shack, when he'd caught her wrist…

"Mom! Are you deaf?"

"Huh?" She shook her head, clearing it of Nick thoughts, poured some coffee for herself, then brought it over to the table. "Sorry, sweetie, what were you saying?"

"Mom, what would you do if Dad moved to Florida?"

"Florida?" Daisy watched her daughter. Emmy's brow was furrowed, and she seemed to be struggling with what she was about to say. She couldn't recall Toby ever mentioning Florida. "Why would he go to Florida?"

Emmy shrugged. "Someone he knows has a restaurant and he could make a whole lot more money, he said."

Daisy immediately understood. Nick had money—or Toby thought so, anyway, and maybe he did. More to the point, though, Toby didn't have money. She smelled manipulation.

"I wouldn't worry too much about it," she said. "I doubt very much he'd leave you—"

"It gets so complicated with Dad sometimes," Emmy interrupted her to say. "Sometimes I feel like I'm the adult and he's this big kid. He gets sad sometimes and...I just feel really bad because I don't know how to help him."

"Oh Em..." Daisy couldn't help her, she wanted to be calm and supportive, but this complex stew of emotions made her eyes fill with tears. She came around the table to sit next to Emmy. "Listen." She pulled her chair up close. "I know exactly how this feels...I went through the same thing with Granddad, but here's the thing. You father *is* an adult and you don't have to carry the burden for him. You can talk to me, we can work things out together, you know that, right?"

Emily nodded.

"It's not disloyal, that's what you're thinking."

"When Granddad acted weird, who did you talk to?"

"No one really. That's why—"

"I can't imagine not having a mom."

"Yeah, well..." Daisy regarded her daughter, whose expression had lightened considerably. Emmy's moods were nothing if not mercurial. "There are probably some days when you think it might not be so bad..."

Emily grinned. "Only *some* days." She got up, threw her arms around Daisy. "Love you," she said, just as the phone rang. "I'll get it." She released Daisy. "Hi Amalia. No, she's right here, just a sec." She handed Daisy the phone. "Amalia."

"I am going to the movies, Daisy," Amalia said. "I thought if you called me you would like to know this."

"The movies?" Daisy sat down at the table. "I thought you said they gave you headaches. Remember, the last time we—"

"Because we were sitting too close," Amalia said. "This time, I shall sit not so close. And afterward, I will be staying with a friend."

"Who?"

"An old friend, I don't think you know her, but I am very happy to see her again."

"Okay," Daisy said slowly. "Call me when you get home. Oh, wait. What are you going to see?" she asked, but Amalia had already hung up.

LATER THAT AFTERNOON, she took Nick's puppy over to the far end of the compound, where the Gypsies were sitting around a trestle table in the shade of a pepper tree making plans for the upcoming Barefoot Festival.

"Another dog?" Bade, the furniture maker, asked.

Daisy shrugged. "Poor little thing, someone just abandoned it. Can you imagine how scared it had to be?"

Around the table, she saw the others exchange looks. She could almost hear the unspoken, "Daisy and her dogs." But they loved her anyway. Unconditional love. Everyone should experience it.

"So," she said, "what's going on with the festival?"

"We've decided we need to take a stand about where they put our stall," Bade said. "Otherwise, we'll be stuck in a corner between the Porta-Potties and lost children."

"We were also saying that you should enter your photographs." Kit gave her a meaningful look. "How about it?"

Daisy made a face.

The framed black and white photographs—portraits of her father, Laguna landscapes, various pets through the ages—hung on the living room wall. She'd made the mistake of saying she'd taken the pictures and then made the bigger mistake of telling Kit she'd taken them and then made the even bigger mistake of admitting that she still dabbled in photography.

"You can do better, Daisy."

"I don't mean to bug you," Kit said. "But the festival is full of stuff that isn't half as good as yours. It just seems such a waste."

"There are bigger tragedies, trust me."

"I'm not saying it's a tragedy—"

"Just drop it, okay?" A glass jug of lemonade was holding down the papers someone had been making notes on. Condensation had blurred the ink. Daisy got up from the table and carried the puppy back toward the cabin. Kit caught up with her.

"You're doing a lot of crying these days," Kit said. "In case you hadn't noticed."

Daisy sniffed. "It's joy. And exultation."

"I know other people's problems are always easier to solve than your own, but if there's anything I can do…"

"Thanks."

"The biographer?"

"Kind of."

"I thought you were just going to tell him no."

"I did. But…" She sighed. "It's hard to explain."

"You don't have to be Superwoman, you know."

"I'm not. Trust me, I'm not."

"Nothing you want to talk about?"

"Nothing, period."

CHAPTER TWELVE

"I LOVED FRANK very much," Amalia said. "He was exciting, he had…" She frowned. "Charisma. He was strong and bold and handsome. But Frank, he was a difficult man."

Nick watched the lights of a boat out on the horizon. They sat on wooden chairs on her small balcony looking out at the ocean. The sun had been going down when he arrived, now it was dark. A candle burned on the table between them illuminating the tape recorder that whirred softly as Amalia reminisced. The answering machine in his apartment had been blinking when he'd returned from an errand. Amelia wanted to see him. Before he could call back, she'd called again. It was very important that they talk, she'd said. It was also important, she'd added, that Daisy not know.

He'd thought of Daisy sitting across the table from him, saw her green eyes. Her smile. The other call on the machine had been Avril, informing him about an increase in Bella's school fees. This on top of the huge chunk of his advance turned over for the cottage in Devon. Money that would have to be returned to the publisher if he abandoned the project. He'd decided then that he would have to live with his conscience.

"Daisy, she idolized him," Amalia said after she'd sat in silence for a while, seemingly lost in her thoughts. "She doesn't see the not so good in him. Daisy sees the good in everyone, even her no-good husband. You have met him? Toby?"

"Yes."

"Not so good, that one. But Daisy says nothing bad, even of him." She put her hand on Nick's arm. "I have thought and thought about this book. At first I thought, yes it will be a good thing. As you get older memories fade, no? You remember only the good things. I thought of all the pictures I have that show the happy times I had with Franky. For Daisy's sake, I talk only of the good things. But it was not all happiness with Frank, you know."

Nick turned his head. Candlelight flickered on her profile; the long straight nose, the upswept mass of hair, mostly gray, woven through with a red chiffon scarf. It wasn't hard to imagine the exotic beauty that must have captivated Frank Truman.

"He had an eye for beautiful women," she said, as though she'd read his thoughts. "I knew what he was doing, but I closed my eyes to it, you know? I don't want to see, so I don't. But then one day, I came here—" she waved her hand "—here to this beach, to this cottage where we are now. I found him with a young woman. They were both naked and running together down to the sea. I remember the sun was shining on her hair and she was laughing and Frank, he looked so happy."

Nick waited. The faint phosphorescent gleam from the breaking waves had an intensity to it that felt like a third presence. As though, he thought, giving rein to his imagination, it represented the artist himself. Earlier, Amalia had brought a heavy shawl from the cabin and wrapped it around her shoulders.

"Are you cold Nick?" she asked.

"No," he lied.

"You are cold." She stood, went inside and returned with a heavy tartan blanket. "Franky wore this," she said as she draped it around his shoulders.

"Thank you."

She sat back down. "I decided I must leave. Franky, he seemed happier with this woman than with me. So I returned to Portugal. After many years, I heard from friends that Franky had a little girl and that he is alone, there is no other woman. I came back then and I stayed until Franky died."

Nick heard the click as the tape came to an end. He turned it over, set the machine to Play. "The fire must have been devastating to you."

"It was. But I think it was more so to Daisy."

"Why do you think that?"

"Because she is less philosophical about life than I am. She and Frank, they had been angry, shouting at each other. And he died before she could say she was sorry. It haunts her."

"She's told you that?"

"I *know* that."

"You're very fond of Daisy, aren't you?"

"She is my daughter. I did not give birth to her, of course, but I love her as if I did."

"She worries about you."

Amalia laughed. "Daisy worries about everybody. It is what I tell you, she sees only the good in people."

"That's not an easy thing to do," Nick said.

"I myself worry about her."

"In what way?

"She keeps things in here." She stabbed at her chest. "She doesn't talk. That's why I think this book is a good thing, to set free all the secrets. But then I think the truth would hurt Daisy too much, and I start thinking maybe it isn't such a good thing."

Nick felt a twinge of alarm. If Amalia changed her mind, the biography was truly doomed. "Do you think the girl in the water with Frank was Daisy's mother?"

"I don't know. Maybe."

"Frank never talked about her?"

"Never. He was a very secretive man. Difficult and

stubborn. Frank, he was never wrong. You could not talk to him. He lived his life as he thought it should be lived, no matter what. I loved him for that." She yawned. "Nicholas, I am tired. If you would like to talk some more tomorrow, that would be all right, but tonight…"

She'd stopped talking, and Nick felt her suddenly tense.

A moment later he understood. Daisy. Slowly emerging from the darkness, her face, in the faint glow of candlelight, tight with anger.

"Don't even try to explain." She looked at Nick, who was coming down the short flight of stairs off the balcony toward her. She took several steps backward. "I don't want to hear anything you have to say." In the dark, she could only see the pale gleam of Amalia's skin, the white of her eyes. "And the next time you crash your dune buggy, don't have the paramedics call me. I don't give a damn. Do whatever you want, drink yourself to death for all I care."

God, no, she didn't mean that. She turned away from them, started back along the beach to the highway. She was running now, tripping over her feet and sobbing so hard her chest hurt. Baba was wrong. Opening your heart didn't lead to forgiveness, it led to hurt and disappointment and…Nick's hand was on her shoulder.

"Go away." She pulled free. "I don't want to talk to you."

"You don't have to talk." He ran along beside her, caught up, then moved in front of her, forcing her to stop. "Daisy. Look at me."

"I don't want to look at you." But she did anyway. His shirt and teeth gleamed white; his hair was dark as the night. "You're traitorous."

"No, I'm not."

"Yes. You are. I said no biography. And you went behind my back."

"*You* said no biography."

"Because I was worried about Amalia. And what do you do? You go and see her anyway. She lied and told me she was going to a movie, and what is she really doing? Talking to you."

"She's a grown woman, Daisy. You can't assume responsibility for other people's lives."

"You—" she poked her finger at his chest "—don't have to worry that she's drinking herself to death."

"Have you tried to help her?"

"Yes."

"That's all you can do, then. You are not responsible for her, Daisy. Any more than you are responsible for Toby. Or your father."

"You don't know." She tried to pull free but he wouldn't release her. "You don't know how things are."

"Why don't you tell me, then?"

"I don't know."

"Try."

"I don't *know*. I don't know what to think."

"Then don't."

"I don't know how to stop."

"Daisy." He caught her face in his hands. "Listen to me. It's all right. Really."

She looked up at his face. *Can I trust you? Should I trust you?* "I don't know what to do. I just want…"

He pulled her into his arms and held on tightly. Minutes passed. Through his shirt, she felt the beat of his heart, the warmth of his skin. She thought of Amalia, probably sitting on the porch still, watching them. She wanted her heart to open the way Baba described it. She thought maybe it had just a bit. Maybe it had started opening last night. Maybe that was why Nick had come into her life. Not just to write about her father but to teach her how to open her heart. She wondered if he'd laugh if she told him that. She decided not to risk it.

"I'm sorry," she said eventually, "for calling you a traitor."

"I've been called worse."

"I'm sure you have."

His arms were still around her, her face against his chest, but she could *feel* him smile. *Happiness is the difference between your reality and your expectations*, Baba had said. *To be happy, accept your reality or adjust your expectations.* Nick's heart beat against her face. Tomorrow, he might let her down. For the moment, just his arms around her seemed like enough.

"Listen," she said, without moving away. "The puppy misses you. If you're not doing anything tomorrow, maybe you could drop by. He'd be happy to see you."

"MOM. HE'S HERE."

Emily burst into the bedroom where Daisy was telling herself that she honestly didn't care what she looked like when Nick got there even though she had emptied two drawers of T-shirts onto the bed and was standing there in jeans and a black bra pulling shirts off hangers and muttering under her breath that she was going to stop eating altogether because she was sick to death of looking so damn fat.

Casually, oh *so* casually, she turned her head to look at her daughter. "Who, sweetie?"

"*Who.*" Emily rolled her eyes. "Like you don't know."

Daisy regarded the shirt she was holding. White cotton, long sleeves, but she'd roll them up. She slipped it on, checked herself out in the mirror.

"Mom, that has a huge stain on the back. And you're wearing a black bra, which totally shows through."

Daisy looked at her daughter. "How did you get to be you?"

"Huh?"

"I mean how could a klutz like me have given birth to someone who knows you don't wear a black bra under a white shirt?"

"You *know* that, Mom. It's just your head's always somewhere else."

Daisy pulled off the shirt. "He's actually here?"

"*Yes*. And get this…" She lowered her voice to a conspiratorial whisper. "He's driving a silver Porsche. Dad is going to go nuts."

"Why?" Daisy paid little attention to cars. Right now she just wanted to find something that didn't make her look like a fat cow. She spotted a pale green sweatshirt down at the end of the row of clothes and pulled it over her head.

"How about this?"

"It's okay," Emily said with a passing glance. "Mom, just find something."

"What about my hair?" Daisy peered into the dresser mirror, experimentally piled it up, holding it in place with one hand. "Up or down?"

"*Mom.*" She ran to the bedroom window. "He's coming up the drive."

"Well, go and talk to him."

"I don't know what to say."

Daisy dropped the fistful of hair and ran a brush through it. She dug in the dresser drawer, hoping to find at least a lipstick, but came up empty. Oh, well.

She straightened her shoulders, eyed her reflection one more time and went out to meet Nick. The dogs, including the new puppy, followed, barking and circling around her. Nick, tall and lanky, was leaning against a low-slung, silver convertible. He wore jeans and a black collarless shirt, managing, somehow, to look both casual and sophisticated. Daisy immediately wanted to run back into the house and change.

She watched him as he crouched to pet the new dog, laughing as the dog licked his face and whimpered trying to climb into his arms.

"You have a very nice new home," he told the dog. "And I don't miss you a bit, so you can stop your performance."

Daisy felt Emmy come up beside her. She turned to smile at her daughter. Emmy had taken the ponytail clip from her hair and brushed it around her shoulders; she was wearing a new blue sweater and lip gloss. *I need to take lessons from my daughter,* Daisy thought.

"You must be Emily," Nick stood and extended his hand. "You've got your mother's green eyes." He paused. "How do you suppose she manages without them?"

Daisy saw Emmy's confusion, then saw her face clear as she caught on to the joke. Emmy grinned and, watching her, Daisy did, too.

"Nick Wynne." A moment passed, and then he

said, "My daughter is twelve. Based on that, I would say you must be around...sixteen?"

Emmy's face glowed. There was no greater compliment than to be told she looked older. Daisy waited for Emily to correct him. When no correction came, Daisy raised an eyebrow.

"I'll be fifteen next September, "she said.

Emmy was smiling shyly, and Daisy knew her daughter had been won over. If Kelsey were there, the two of them would be hungrily absorbing details to compare later. "*His eyes were, like, exactly the same blue as your sweater,*" and "*Did you hear the way he said...*" and "*Omigod, he looks exactly like...*" In fact, Daisy thought, he did look a little like someone she'd seen on TV, but she couldn't think who it was.

Nick was telling Emmy a story about something the puppy had done in his apartment, and Emmy was smiling: clearly captivated. *If only I could get her to listen to me that attentively.* She wondered how all this looked to Nick. Should she show him the goats? Would he think she was some sort of wacko California nature freak with her vegetable garden and chickens? Did she care what he thought?

Emmy and Nick were talking about his car. Was it a Porsche Carrera, Emmy wanted to know, and Nick had turned to look at the car, as though maybe it had morphed into a Pontiac while his back was turned. "Rented," he said with a shrug. "For the day. Part of the California experience," he added with a glance in Daisy's direction. Meeting his eyes, Daisy felt her face flush.

"Driving along the coast with the top down, wind in the hair, that sort of thing." He smiled. "Perhaps it's a bit of a cliché though."

"It's cool," Emmy said.

"I'd offer to take you for a ride," he said to Emily. "But, as you can see, there are only two seats and I don't know whether your mother would approve…"

"Maybe another time," Daisy said.

"Oh, come *on*, Mom."

"I'm actually quite a safe driver," Nick said. "Very safe really."

"Do you drive a Porsche Carrera in England?"

He smiled slightly.

"Or…what's the ostentatious equivalent? A Rolls-Royce. Do you drive your daughter around in a Rolls?"

"Mom, stop it." Emmy shot a look at Nick. "My mom gets these weird ideas."

"That's all right." He addressed Daisy. "Your point being that the Porsche represents—"

"Conspicuous consumption."

"Oh, please." Emmy shook her head. "Like I don't see Porsches every day. Dad's always pointing them out."

Nick winked at her. "I'll bring the Ford next time,"

he said, then opened the trunk of the Porsche and brought out the dog basket and a paper bag with a pet shop logo on the front. He handed Daisy the bag. She glanced inside. Rubber squeak toys—a hot dog and a hamburger with lemon-colored cheese and lime-green lettuce.

Nick was watching her. "You're smiling."

"I know." She couldn't seem to stop. "I guess something struck me funny about you shopping for dog toys."

"I told you she was weird," Emmy said.

Nick returned to the car and came back with a box of chocolates, which he handed to Emily and a bottle of wine. He held it out to Daisy like an offering. "You did mention dinner? I thought you had, but then I wondered if it wasn't just wishful thinking."

A Fig Newton of your imagination. It was something her father used to say. "Nope," she said. "I invited you." And then she met her daughter's eyes. Emmy had walked into the kitchen early that morning to find Daisy in the middle of paring the spikes from a bowlful of nopal cactus paddles.

"I'm not eating those." Emmy had firsthand experience with Daisy's culinary experiments and knew that, except for poisonous stuff, nothing that grew in the ground was too offbeat for Daisy to put on the table.

"I'm not asking you to," Daisy had said.

"You're not making them for that Nick guy?"

"As a matter of fact, I am."

"Cactus?"

"*Ensalada de nopalitos*. Don't knock it till you try it."

"I wouldn't try it if you paid me," Emmy had said.

Now Emmy was grinning widely and shooting sideways glances at Nick, who was smiling too. "Let me guess," he said. "Dinner burned up?"

Emmy laughed. "You *wish*."

"Hmm." Nick thought for a moment. "Is it something…strange?"

"You could say that," Emmy shot back.

"There's a chef on the telly who supposedly eats snake hearts…"

"Ooh, yuck."

"Kind of makes cactus sound good, doesn't it?" Daisy grabbed the wicker dog basket. "Come on, I'll show you around."

"I've got to go," Emmy said. "I'm having dinner with my dad."

"Not cactus, I assume."

She shook her head. "No way."

"Well, I very much enjoyed meeting you."

"Me, too." She blushed. "I mean I enjoyed meeting you, too."

"Emily," he called as she started down the path to the cabin. "I meant to ask. Have you named the puppy yet?"

Emily glanced at Daisy. "Elvis?"

Daisy laughed. That choice had come *way* out of left field. "Sure, why not?"

"'Cause he ain't nothing but a hound dog," Nick sang in a terrible parody of a Texas accent.

"Very nice girl," Nick said after Emmy left. "Pretty, too. Like her mother."

"Thank you, kind sir," Daisy said, making a mockery out of the compliment because she was no good at that kind of stuff. Plus, she couldn't help wondering if all of this—acting like a date almost— was genuine or just a way of warming her up to talk about her father. Even if she asked him straight out, he could lie, so there was no point in that, and it would probably come off all paranoid and insecure. *You couldn't possibly like me for me, you must want something else.*

IT WAS ALMOST DARK by the time she'd given Nick the fifty-cent tour, another of her father's expressions. Nick had been full of questions. If he wasn't really interested, he was a damn good actor. He'd asked to see the work of the artists living in the other cabins. She'd told him that in fact, she had a lot of their pieces—pottery, watercolors, fabric—in her own cabin. What she didn't mention was that almost all of it was in payment for rent. And the fires burning everywhere, he'd wondered, did she ever worry about wildfires? They were a part of life, she'd told him. You just have to get on with it. And the goats: he'd had all kinds of questions about the goats. Where exactly did she take them to graze? Did she make goat cheese? He'd had some excellent goat cheese in Greece. Were there any animals she didn't like? Was she scared of snakes? Had she ever found any on the property?

She'd answered that she loaded the herd into the truck, drove up to various hillside homes whose owners contracted her to remove the grasses, that she did sometimes make cheese, that she couldn't think of an animal she could possibly dislike and, yes, she'd found all kinds of snakes, but most of them weren't poisonous and, no, she wasn't scared.

Now they were in the kitchen, three of the dogs, including Elvis, drifting around, and Nick was sitting backward on one of the bentwood chairs, his arms wrapped around the back, his chin propped on the wooden support. The cactus paddles were in a bowl in the fridge, but she'd pretty much given up on the idea of serving them—a cactus salad had seemed interesting and exotic when she'd first thought of it; now it just seemed weird and unappetizing.

"What do you like to eat?" she asked, mentally running through the contents of her freezer.

"Snake hearts," he said solemnly.

"Freezer's full of them. Any particular preference? Adders? Grass snakes?"

"I'm rather partial to garter snakes, actually."

"Uh-huh." She eyed him briefly. "You look the garter snake type."

"I could be wrong," he said, "but I don't think that was a compliment."

She thought about offering him some wine. There was a half bottle of chardonnay that she and Kit had started one night and some Chianti left over from the Gypsy's Italian potluck. Both were the cheap supermarket variety that Martin wouldn't drink if you paid him. And then she remembered the wine Nick had left on the table. She opened it, poured two glasses and set one down in front of him.

"Cheers." Still standing, she clinked her glass against his. "You look…contemplative. Like you're sitting there, coming up with questions to ask me, but you're just waiting for the right moment to start firing away."

"I was waiting until the wine took effect," he said. "My thought was to get you good and sloshed first."

"On one bottle?"

"I didn't want to scare you. There's a dozen more bottles in the boot."

She held her glass by the stem, swishing the wine around. Watched the way it clung to the sides of the glass. Legs, her father had told her, were an indication of quality wine. Children in Europe drank wine with dinner, he'd said as he poured her a small glass. She'd hated it. Who cared what children in Europe drank. She was an American, she'd wanted milk.

"This is a very comfortable room." Nick was now moving about the kitchen, picking up this, examining that. Pots of herbs on the windowsill, copper pans hanging from a rack over the stove, a shelf overflowing with cookbooks. "You obviously enjoy… this sort of thing."

"Cooking?" She leaned back against the counter. "I guess my hips kind of gave that away, huh?"

"Your hips are…" He seemed to struggle not to smile, then gave up. "Engaging a woman in discussion about any of her body parts is moving onto dangerous territory. I know that from experience. But your hips are…very nice."

Daisy cackled. "I love it." She wanted to tweak his cheeks. "You're so sweet, Nick. *Very nice hips*."

He peered into his wine. "The rest of you is quite nice, too."

"Thanks. But don't overdo it. I'll figure you've got ulterior motives."

He drank some wine, set down his glass. Picked it up again. "So," he finally said, "what happened to the cactus?"

It took her a minute. "Oh, the cactus. I took it off the menu."

"Why?"

"You're not telling me you actually want cactus?"

"I was rather looking forward to it. I'd like to see it prepared."

She searched his face for clues that he wasn't just stringing her along, but he actually looked quite interested—the bright, alert kid at the front of the class. "I usually grill it lightly," she said. "I prefer that to steaming, which can make it kind of slimy."

He nodded as though she'd given him the secret to the universe. Moments passed. The parrot squawked. The refrigerator hummed. She folded her arms across her chest and quickly unfolded them. It looked defensive. One hand on her hip—no, too provocative. Both hands on hips—no, drew attention. She drank some more wine.

"*Nopal* means 'cactus' in Spanish," she said, after what seemed like five minutes had dragged by. "*Nopales* is the stem. *Nopalitos* are what the big pads are called when they're cut up and cooked."

"Ah," he said slowly. "I see. Very interesting. So the…um prickles?"

"I cut them off," Daisy said. "Or you could use them for toothpicks."

Nick laughed politely.

"And you chop it all up and mix it with avocado and chilies and *queso fresco*, which is this white Mexican cheese, and, Nick, what I'm really wondering is whether you're here to be with me, or if this is just a way to try to get information about my father." She downed the rest of her wine. "Not that I didn't appreciate you holding me last night because I did. I really did. Like I said though, I'm just wondering."

"Funny thing is, I was wondering about something, too," Nick said. "Last night on the beach. Did you want me to hold you because you were cold, or…"

Daisy smiled. "I'm not cold now," she said softly.

"And?"

"I'd still like you to hold me."

"I can do even better than that," he said.

CHAPTER THIRTEEN

TOBY WAS IN LEAH'S box of a kitchen trying to do something with the frozen lasagna he'd taken from her freezer—*frozen* lasagna, go figure. *She's invited* his *daughter to dinner and he's only the chef of the hottest restaurant in Laguna Beach and she's serving* his *daughter frozen damn lasagna.* In the living room, he could hear Emmy nattering on to Leah about Mr. Fancy Ass Biographer, whom she hadn't stopped talking about ever since he'd picked her up. First, it was the Porsche, which she didn't need to tell him about because he'd already seen it parked at the side of the road, but she'd gone on about it anyway.

He sprinkled garlic salt—naturally, Leah didn't have fresh garlic—over the top of the lasagna. Then he found the green box of fake parmesan cheese, which he was always telling Leah she shouldn't waste her money on and wished to hell Emmy wasn't there so he could smoke a little weed to calm down.

"You know who he looks like?" Emmy was saying to Leah. "That guy on the Travel Channel—"

"Omigod I know who you're going to say," Leah squealed. "Anthony Bourdain. You know what's so weird? I told him that when he came into the restaurant looking for Daisy."

"Wow," Emmy said.

"*Wow*," Toby mimicked. "*Isn't that just so bitching keen?*"

"Do you think he likes your mom?" Leah asked.

Emmy giggled. "You know what, I think he kind of does."

"How cool," Leah said. "He's so cute, too."

"I think she likes him, too," Emmy said. "She never fixes herself up or anything, but, like, today when he was coming over she was going nuts looking for stuff to wear and, I don't know, the way she was looking at him…"

"You can just tell, huh?"

"And he rescued this dog, so of course that scores him points. His name is Elvis and, it was so cute, I came up with the name and Nick sang, 'He ain't nothing but a hound dog,' except that he has this English accent."

"*So* cute." Leah sighed.

Toby wanted to barf. Women were so damn stupid, even—he hated to say it—his own daughter. Anyone with half a brain could see that Daisy and Mr. Fancy Pants had zip going for each other. Still, it hacked him off anyway. He went to Leah's fridge and got a beer. Cheap generic stuff that tasted like spit. "I'm not Daisy," Leah had said last night when he'd bitched about the kind of beer she bought. "I don't have millions in the bank."

He popped the beer. Maybe it wasn't just stuff on Daisy's dad Mr. Slimy Limey wanted. Maybe he was after Daisy's money. And if Daisy was too dumb to see that, maybe someone needed to set her straight.

"…and his daughter's name is Bella," Emmy was saying. "Isn't that such a cute name?"

"Way cute," Leah agreed. "So anyway, you wanna watch *The Apprentice*? I've got DVDs of all the shows."

"HE HAD THIS JACKET with leather-covered buttons." Nick turned to look at Daisy. They were settled in front of the fireplace in her cabin, the room in darkness except for the candle she'd lit hours earlier on the mantel, and the flames roaring up the chimney. "D'you know the kind I mean?"

She nodded. "Like little footballs."

"Yes. And the jacket was an odd color, sort of a cinnamon, ginger…rather like your hair really. Not that I'm calling your hair—"

"I know what you're saying." She touched his arm. "Go on."

"Well, it was scratchy and rough and I remember as a small boy, I disliked him picking me up or doing anything that brought my face close to the cloth. Yet after he walked out, I'd sit in the bottom of the closet where his clothes were, with the jacket wrapped around me, just sort of breathing in…his essence, I suppose."

"Ah." Daisy had her feet curled under her and she regarded him, her face solemn. "That's such a sad story."

"It's much better with violin music."

"Stop it." She smacked his knee. "I'm serious. So he just walked away and you never heard from him again?"

"I heard from my mother, a year or so before she herself died, that he'd been found dead in a boarding house. Up north, in Blackpool, of all places. He'd apparently had a heart attack and the landlady found him in his bed." He yawned and glanced at his watch. "It's getting late. I should probably go."

"You probably should," Daisy agreed, but neither of them made any move. "It's weird. I think you're secretly here to get me to talk about my dad and we end up talking about yours."

She straightened her legs, pulled off her boots. Nick reached for one of them. Small, almost a child's size, yet tough and well worn. Her toes pointed up, the red socks she wore dark, almost the color of coal in the firelight. He turned onto his side, propped his head on one hand and watched the flames dance and spark.

"I think it's rather like a jigsaw. The whole thing

about your father's biography or at least my need and motivation to write it. My father was gone for most of my life, which is probably why I've been such a dismal failure with Bella. And then there was your father, or at least the father I imagined must have painted that picture of you, and somewhere in there I have this sense that if I could work it all out, find a pattern to the pieces, I'd understand..."

"Understand? Yourself?"

"I suppose that's what I'm saying."

"My father wasn't everything you read into that picture," Daisy said. "I mean he wasn't all bad, but if you're imagining that our life together was one long, sunny day at the beach, it wasn't that either."

"No, I realize that." Amalia had alluded to Truman's anger, his temperament. As had the gallery owner. Daisy herself had shown him the haunting images she'd photographed—stunning work, which her father had cruelly derided. She reached for another log, tossed it on the glowing coals. He watched the wood turn the color of the sunset he and Daisy had seen together. Frank's house could have been burned down by one of the wildfires, Max Bowen had said, or someone could have just struck a match.

Earlier in the evening, as they were washing dishes together after dinner she'd asked him about the biography.

"What was it about my dad? As opposed to some other artist?"

He'd set the glass he was drying down on the counter. "Well, his work of course. I was intrigued by the *Innocence* portrait—"

"You mean you liked it?" Daisy, as always, had headed directly for the point.

"Aesthetically, it's not really my style," he'd confessed. "I go more for abstract—"

"That figures."

"How so?"

"Because abstracts are…difficult to pin down," she'd said. She'd reached past him to pick up the glass he'd set down. "You can read whatever you want into them."

He'd taken a moment to consider her answer, was still pondering when Daisy had stuck her face up under his. "Hey."

"Tell me what you're thinking this very moment." Daisy's voice broke into his reverie.

"I was thinking about you," he replied truthfully.

The candle had burned down, melted into a molten tangerine pool in its clear glass container. Music had been playing on the stereo all evening, jazzy, background stuff that he'd tuned in and out. "I saw you there one wonderful day," a woman, Ella Fitzgerald maybe, sang. "You took my heart and threw it away…"

"Your music?" he asked now. "I mean, this is the kind of thing you play on your car stereo, for instance?"

"No, this is my seduction music."

He turned his head to look at her.

"Just kidding. It's my dad's music. Kind of schmaltzy, I guess, but I like it sometimes."

"'What Is this Thing Called Love?'" Nick said, naming the song. His own musical tastes were on the schmaltzy side, he supposed.

"Good question," Daisy said.

"That's the name—"

She smacked the top of his head. "Duh."

He grinned.

"But it *is* a good question," Daisy said.

"Do you have an answer?"

"Nope."

A log shifted and she got on all fours, scooting over to poke it back into the fireplace. Still on her hands and knees, she turned to him, yawned ostentatiously, then looked straight into his eyes. "You're probably the most interesting, best-looking guy that's sat by this fireplace for…a looooooong time, and if you weren't doing that damn biography, I'd take your hand and lead you into the bedroom."

Her hair hung around her shoulders like curtains. Nick could see yellow flickers of flame in her eyes. He caught a strand of her hair, tugged at it. "I would allow myself to be led."

She sat up, wrapped her arms around her knees. "Really?"

"Really."

"But it probably wouldn't be a very good idea."

"Probably not."

"Plus Emmy will be home soon."

"She's not spending the night with Toby?"

Daisy shook her head. "Seriously, though, Nick, you're not bad...I'm not very good with mushy stuff, but that's kind of like saying, you're..."

"Not bad?"

They both laughed.

"You're not bad yourself, Ms. Daisy Fowler." Nick kissed her once on the mouth, then he stood, pulling her up with him. His arm around her waist, he walked with her to the front door. Cool, damp air rushed in when he opened it. Fog hovered above the eucalyptus.

"Good night, Daisy."

AFTER NICK LEFT, she stood at the window until the pinkish blur of his taillights disappeared in the night. The fire was almost out and she couldn't decide whether to build it back up or go to bed. She should call Amalia. Amalia had called her that morning, but she hadn't felt much like talking to her then, and she didn't feel any more like it now. She wanted to think about Nick.

Nick and bed. Nick in bed. Nick in bed with her.

She raked at her hair. I want him. *I haven't wanted anything like that for the longest time, and now I do.* "Why can't I have him?" She felt like stamping her foot.

The phone rang. She answered on the second ring. Toby.

"Emmy's going to sleep over here at Leah's," he said. "Okay?"

"Fine." She wanted to cry. "I'll pick her up—"

"Nick still there?"

"Is that any of your business?" She hung up the phone.

Nick was…seductive. Not just in a physical sense but in the way he'd somehow lured her into talking about her father almost without realizing what she was doing. She stripped off her clothes and pulled on soft, warm sweats. But if telling Nick about her father were a banquet, all she'd done was feed him a few appetizers.

FOUR DAYS LATER, Nick stood at the imitation-granite-topped counter of his apartment kitchen cutting an apple into quarters. He was thinking about his daughter. When Bella visited him in London, every other weekend unless he was out of town on assignment—which happened more often than he wanted to admit to himself—he would spend the previous day cleaning up the flat and buying food to stock the refrigerator.

Even then, she'd complain that he didn't keep the sort of things children wanted to eat. After she left, the place always looked as though it had been burglarized. He couldn't recall a time when he hadn't had a panicked call from her the next day to say she'd left her absolutely favorite skirt or book or shoes and would he please, please, drop them by because there was simply no way she could live without them.

Once it had been a red cardigan. Not one of her favorites apparently because there had been no call about it. She'd left it on the back of a chair, where it had stayed for weeks. He hadn't brought it to her attention because he liked seeing it there, a bright burst of crimson in his black and white world.

He'd been thinking about Bella when he'd bought the pot of red geraniums yesterday. Now, as he picked off a withered leaf, his thoughts moved on to Frank Truman. Or, more specifically, Frank Truman's biography.

And, more specifically still, to the fact that nothing was happening with the biography. A great black bird of doubt and negativity had perched on his shoulder, second-guessing every thought he tried to express in writing, mocking tentative conclusions, even tearing apart work he'd thought

already completed. It accompanied him everywhere: early morning jogs, sunset walks along the
beach, the balcony of the Hotel Laguna. Last night
he'd drunk a second, then a third glass of wine,
hoping to relax into sleep and, perhaps, wake re-
freshed and inspired. Instead he had a mild
hangover and the bird hadn't budged.

Perhaps he should just call Daisy and explain that
she was getting in the way of him thinking clearly
and objectively about her father. Which, he supposed,
might be a tad premature since she hadn't actually
clarified her position on the biography. There was
just this tacit understanding. Or at least he felt the existence of a tacit understanding.

Maybe that was part of the problem—the absence
of a signed contact from Daisy agreeing to tell or,
failing that, a handshake. A kiss. Sealed with a kiss.
He went to the balcony and looked out at the water.
The air smelled faintly of smoke. Fires continued to
erupt daily. Four houses in a hilltop enclave here,
three more in a canyon community there. No fires of
inspiration though. No blazing eruptions of insight,
no smoldering desire to get to work each day

Last night, he'd decided to confront Daisy with
the gallery owner's comments. Call her on the phone.

"It's all perfectly ludicrous," he would say. "I'll
state that right up front. But, well, this whole
business about...well, no, let me rephrase that, this

idiotic idea that you shot your father and then set the house on fire to cover things up. Ridiculous, I know. Look, I can hardly say it with a straight face. Rubbish, I agree. Why would he even make such a comment?"

He'd asked the fire chief the same thing. That man had shrugged. "This is fire country," he'd said. "Nature never intended people to fill chaparral-covered hillsides with multi-million-dollar homes."

And Daisy's ex-husband. Now there was a chap who wouldn't think twice about striking a match. And her stepmother. What if Amalia, after an evening with the gin bottle, had just decided Frank had to go?

Maybe he should drop by and see Daisy. Posit all these questions and, after they'd straightened everything out, fall into bed and make mad, passionate love. That, come to think of it, was probably the best idea he'd had all day.

God. He went back into the kitchen, took a carton of orange juice from the fridge, downed half of it—chastising himself for being too lazy to squeeze the fresh oranges that were everywhere for the taking. Then he wandered out to the balcony once more, watched the ocean glimmer, watched the passing parade of lovely young things on Rollerblades, grew bored and came back inside.

He switched on the telly.

"Now that the embers have cooled," an announcer

said, "residents have been returning, tentatively, to the canyon here, not knowing what would be left. Most are trying to see if anything can be salvaged. For the few whose homes survived, the experience places them in an unsettling middle ground between relief and anguish."

When the phone rang, he nearly fell over himself in his eagerness to answer it.

"Dude," Toby said. "Long time no see. What's shaking?"

It took Nick a moment to rally. He'd hoped it was Daisy calling. Or Bella, who, when he'd called her the night before, had cut short their conversation— she was expecting a very important call from her best friend—but promised to ring back. She hadn't.

"The usual," he said. "Work. At least trying to work."

"Hey, just say if I'm bugging you."

"No, no," Nick reassured him, truthfully. "Any distraction gratefully accepted."

"Yeah, well, anyway, seeing as it's Monday, Wildfire's closed, so I'm off the hook," Toby said. "I'm feeling like doing something. You want to see the old man's house? Not the house that burned down, but where it used to be? I've got this buggy that can take the hills like nothing flat."

THIRTY MINUTES LATER, his nose and mouth full of the dust, Nick was sitting in the passenger seat of Toby's

Jeep, tearing up a steep cattle trail just off Laguna Canyon Road as if the cavalry were in hot pursuit— and wondering, belatedly, at Toby's real motivation for inviting him. A convenient tumble off the cliff and the ex-wife's new admirer would be competition no more.

"Awesome, huh?" Toby shot a glance at Nick. Aviator sunglasses and the bill of his baseball cap hid the top half of his face, but the wide grin left little doubt that bouncing through Laguna's back country was infinitely preferable to slaving over a hot stove. "D'you ever hear of some guy called Timothy Leary?"

"Turn on, tune in, drop out," Nick said. He'd probably been about five when Leary was getting disaffected middle-class kids to quit school, head to California and drop acid, but he remembered in his early teens reading about and feeling vaguely envious of Leary's nose-thumbing, counterculture life. "What about him?"

"He and a bunch of these hippy potheads hid out from police right over there." Toby used one arm to wrestle the Jeep back onto the path from where it had jumped a hair-raising few inches from the edge of a hillside. "Back up there a ways, there used to be these three houses they lived in and dealt drugs from."

"They're not there now?"

"Nah. Long gone." He slowed the Jeep to a crawl and gazed over at the site. "*Wild* times. All the pot in the world."

"So Truman's house…" Nick prompted. Toby had leaned over to search through the glove box, perhaps about to suggest a little herbal supplement right now, Nick thought.

"Right *up.*" He pointed at the Leary site. "Stone's throw away. Exact same conditions fire-wise right now as it was then. No rain for months, bone-dry chaparral. One match, that's all it takes. Four hundred homes burned that year. It looked like it was going to burn right down the hills into town. Half a billion dollars."

He cut the ignition, folded his hands behind his head. "They arrested this one guy who said he started one of the fires somewhere, but it turned out to be some whacko who was in a Mexican jail the day the fire broke out."

"Clever way to cover up a crime," Nick said, casting an exploratory line. "If you were that way inclined."

"You got that right," Toby agreed. "Arson's a tough nut to crack."

"Do they ever catch the culprits?" Nick asked.

Toby shrugged. "They've caught a few. Somebody sees a license plate, or someone who's not too swift can't get the device to ignite properly, drops it off thinking it's gonna go *zoom* in ten or fifteen minutes and takes off down the road. But then it doesn't go off and the thing's covered in fingerprints. Those wooden cabins of Daisy's, though, would go up like a rocket…"

"You worry about her, do you?" Nick stretched his legs out, mimicking Toby's casual posture. "Wild-fires and that sort of thing…"

"Daisy's a big girl."

Nick watched a hawk circle lazily, high overhead under a sapphire sky. From where they sat at the crest of the hill, he could see Laguna, like a toy village down below, and beyond it the glittering strip of Pacific Ocean. Toby was searching in the glove box and found what he was looking for. It wasn't a joint.

"Ever use one of these?" Sunlight glittered off the barrel of the small handgun he held out for Nick's inspection. "I keep telling Daisy she needs one. Living out on a dirt road with a bunch of weirdos. Know what I mean?"

CHAPTER FOURTEEN

WHEN A WEEK WENT by and she still hadn't heard from Nick, Daisy decided to hell with him, anyway. "'Got along without him before I met him,'" she sang as she dug around in one of the bathroom cabinets, trying to find the one-pound plastic margarine tub where she stored her makeup. "'Gonna get along without him now.'"

Not that she hadn't come up with a few pretty good reasons to at least give *him* a call. "Emily wants to be a biographer when she grows up (Emily wasn't aware of this yet), and she wondered if you could give her some career advice." Or, "Elvis has gone off his food. I think he might be pining for you. Want me to bring him over?" Even, "I've developed a new and improved cactus salad recipe…" No, scratch that one. No more luring guys with food. It didn't work anyway.

"Hey, Mom," Emmy called from the living room. "I let Deanna out of her cage and she's sitting on Elvis's back."

"Don't let her drop sunflower seeds all over the

living room—I just vacuumed," Daisy yelled back. A broken heart could make you pretty industrious. She'd also done three loads of laundry, raked out the goats' pen and relined the kitchen cabinets. It wasn't even noon. "And don't let Elvis pee on the carpet again."

She found the margarine tub and pried off the plastic lid. The cap from a lipstick had come off and a pill, aspirin probably, was lodged inside the tube. She tried to reach for it with her thumb and forefinger, but couldn't get it. She carried the tub and the lipstick into the kitchen. In the living room, Emmy was stretched out on the couch watching *Miracle Makeover*, the puppy asleep on her chest, the parrot stepping daintily through her hair. "Check this out." She nodded at the TV as Daisy passed by. "This woman looked totally old and ugly. Look at her now...wait, she's gonna come out in a dress from some place in Beverly Hills."

Daisy spread the contents of the margarine tub out over the kitchen table. A tube of Mossy Glen eye shadow had also lost its cap. The eye shadow had oozed out, covering everything else in the tub with a sticky surface of Mossy Glen.

"Mom, really, you've got to see this," Emmy called. "She looks awesome."

Daisy carried the tub back through the living room, stopped long enough to see a woman with long, smooth, corn-color hair and a glittery gown disappear into the arms of a big, burly guy in jeans and a flannel shirt.

"That's her husband," Emmy said. "Look, he's crying."

"He's probably figuring she'll want to start eating at the Ritz instead of McDonald's," Daisy said.

Back in the bathroom, she rummaged through some drawers looking for makeup she knew she'd stashed away somewhere. Rewarded with a tortoise shell compact of blush, she experimented with a smear of pink powder across her cheeks, applying it with her fingers since the brush had gone AWOL. She vaguely recalled using it to apply an egg wash when she couldn't find her pastry brush. Now she eyed herself in the bathroom mirror, wet her index finger, rubbed it over some of the dried Mossy Glen on the underside of the compact and spread it across her eyelids. Then she removed the rubber band from her ponytail, brushed out her hair so it fell loosely around her shoulders and took another look at herself in the mirror. Hmm.

"So, Nick, like what you see?"

She went into the living room. Emmy had the puppy's front paws in both hands and was making him do a little jig on her chest. "'I ain't nothing but a hound dog,'" she sang.

"Don't sing that," Daisy said, without stopping to think first.

"How come?" Emily rolled her head to look at Daisy, then did a double take. "What d'you do to your face?"

"I just put a little makeup on. How does it look?"

Emmy sighed. Her expression turned to one of pity. "Mom, you *totally* need a makeover. That makeup's, like, way older than I am."

"You're probably right." Daisy went into the bathroom and washed her face. A makeover might be a good idea. Not just for Nick because, to be honest, after thinking things over for a week, she still didn't know whether he'd been using her to get information, or whether he was madly in love with her. Well, okay, that was going too far, but maybe whether he might like her. She was so out of circulation, so out of practice, she had no idea, but this might be a good start.

The phone rang. *Nick. Please let it be Nick.*

"Daisy," Amalia said. "Have you heard from Nicholas?"

"Have you?"

"No. I left him a message, but he doesn't call."

"That's the kind of guy he is, I guess."

"WELL IT WAS at a standstill a few days ago," Nick told his agent, who had called to inquire how the biography was going. "Now it's dead in its tracks." He described the unnerving Jeep ride with Toby. "Clearly, he meant the gun as a warning."

"Are you concerned for your personal safety?"

"Good Lord, no," Nick said. "Happens on a daily basis. Ex-husbands brandishing guns at me." He leaned back in his chair, stuck his feet up on the table, narrowly managing to avoid toppling a glass of water into the computer keyboard. "*Concerned* would be overstating things a bit. I do think he's a bit of a loose cannon, though."

"Maybe it's another piece of the jigsaw," Rod said. "Didn't someone tell you Truman kept guns? Maybe the ex-husband shot Truman then lit the fire to cover up?"

Nick considered. It was difficult to contemplate without putting Daisy in the picture, though, which raised more questions. Had she known? Were she and Amalia in cahoots? "Anything's possible, I suppose. But I'm a biographer, not a detective."

"So Truman's daughter," Rod asked, "what do think she saw in this Toby character in the first place? Just wanted to defy Daddy?"

"Something along those lines. Truman was, at best, impossibly exacting. She could never satisfy him even when she tried, so maybe she decided to give him something to really complain about."

HE WAS STILL THINKING about Daisy some twenty minutes after he'd ended the call with Rod. Her own explanation for marrying Toby—emotional support after her father died and the daughter she and Toby had had together didn't entirely satisfy him. He found it far more convincing that by continuing to tolerate and even support Toby after all these years, she was in some way still getting back at her father.

What he couldn't achieve, ironic given the review of his last biography, was the emotional detachment to objectively look at the whole picture. In need of an excuse not to write, he strolled over to Wild Oregano, a health food supermarket—the only grocery of any sort within walking distance—where he'd bought orange juice and, once, a jar of ersatz coffee that was so awful it drove him to a coffee shop in search of a decent cup to start his day.

The store itself was a work of art, with rainbow piles of fruit and vegetables stacked high along one wall and zinc buckets full of flowers in kaleidoscopic arrangements. Wooden tubs were filled with rice, barley and various grains and exotically named beans that he wouldn't have the foggiest idea how to cook, although he imagined Daisy would. What, for example, did one do with an adzuki bean?

He should try to cook dinner for himself, but he couldn't think of anything he might cook that he'd then enjoy eating. Playing it safe, he filled his basket with food that required no cooking to make it edible: tomatoes, avocados, a loaf of bread. If nothing else, he'd at least have a sandwich with his beer.

He paid for the food and, paper bag in hand, started across Coast Highway when he heard a scream. He turned to see a tiny, white-haired woman sprawled out across the grassy strip, groceries spilled all over the place. He set his own bag down and rushed over to the old woman, kneeling in front of her. Other than appearing shaken, she seemed fine.

"All right?" he asked. "No broken bones?"

She shook her head, smiled weakly and allowed him to help her to her feet. He held up his hand to stop the flow of traffic down the Coast Highway and, arm-in-arm, they slowly progressed across the road to a seat on one of the benches facing the ocean.

"You're very kind," she said.

"I'm on foot," Nick said, "but I'd be glad to walk you somewhere."

She shook her head. "My daughter is just over there. She told me to wait for her but...independence is a hard habit to break. She went into one of those shops." She fluttered a hand in the direction of the market he'd just left. "I'll sit here and wait for her."

"Would you like me to wait with you?"

"I'm sure you have more to do than keep an old lady company," she said sweetly. "Thank you, I'll be just fine."

Nick wished her well and waited at the curb for the light to change.

"Dogs, old women..." a voice beside him said. "Is there no end to your goodness?"

"It is infinite," Nick, suddenly ridiculously happy, turned to look at Daisy. "And what a fortunate coincidence you were there to witness it."

"No such thing as a coincidence," Daisy said.

They were on the ocean side of the highway now, standing beneath the branches of a massive tree whose gnarly, fingerlike roots splayed out around the perimeter of the trunk. Daisy's hair fell like silk around the shoulders of her yellow sweater. She looked different, but he couldn't quite pinpoint how. He couldn't think of a thing to say.

"Did you know that?" she asked.

"Know what?" His brain finally clicked into gear. "The coincidence thing? No, I um..." Not even remotely given to mysticism, he once again found himself at a loss for words. Still, he gave it a try. "You didn't *just* appear, you mean?"

"No."

"So the explanation then—"

"You're not supposed to try to analyze this stuff, but..." She grinned. "I do anyway. Maybe I was supposed to see that you have this good and kind side and that I should trust you. And I did, until I figured out that you weren't going to call me again."

"Right. Uh, about that..."

"You broke your dialing finger? Those things on the end of your arms are just painted on?"

He laughed and made a show of checking his hands. Then he said, "I started to find it very difficult to work. And I thought it might help to keep my distance for a bit."

"Did it help?"

"Not really. Work has all but ground to a halt."

"Wow." Her smile faded. "I'm sorry. If it's my fault, I mean."

"It's not your fault," he said, which wasn't entirely true. Perhaps *fault* was the wrong word, though. Daisy had served to confuse things, which was as much his fault for allowing himself to be drawn in. And then he suddenly realized what was different about her. "It's your hair."

"My hair? That's why you can't work?"

"You've guessed it," he said solemnly. "Your hair haunts my dreams."

"Seriously."

"Seriously, my thoughts were going off in one direction and my mouth in another. I just meant to say, you hair looks very nice."

She raised a hand to touch the side of her head. "I had it straightened."

Nick nodded. Women baffled him. None of them was ever satisfied, it seemed to him, with the way things were. Daisy with straight hair looked different from Daisy with curly hair, but he honestly couldn't say one was an improvement over the other. Although she did look very attractive, more glossy and put together, so perhaps straightening had some effect beyond the obvious.

"It looks nice," he repeated. "Very nice."

"Thanks," she said. "I guess."

He raised an eyebrow.

"Well, okay, I had this complete makeover. See—" she pulled her hair back from her face "—eyebrow wax, new makeup, mine was older than Emily, she brought that to my attention. Skin peel. God, why am I telling you all this?" She grinned. "I am *so* bad at girly stuff."

If he hadn't been on the verge of falling for Daisy before, Nick thought, he may have just heard the crash. Every woman he'd ever known had in one way or another encouraged him to believe that looking beautiful was as natural as falling out of bed. The morning light invariably proved this false, but somehow they perpetuated the myth and he, like most men, just went on buying it. Now here was Daisy, casually refuting the whole charade. It was all he could do not to take her in his arms. Biography be damned. Financial pressures would, of course, bring him to his senses. Just not now.

"Where are you off to now?" he asked.

She jiggled the paper sack she was carrying. "Lemons. Gotta go make desserts."

"At the restaurant?"

"Yep."

He thought of Toby. After making the remark about Daisy needing a gun for her protection, Toby had just returned his to the glove box. The gun had clearly been another warning, though. Stay away from my woman, even if we do happen to be divorced. He looked at Daisy with her bag of lemons and wanted to forbid her to see Toby again, which, of course, was patently ridiculous. Still he felt distinctly uneasy.

"How late will you be there?" he asked.

"Oh, I'm just going to whip up a couple of desserts, then I'm taking off."

"And Toby?" he asked, trying to sound casual and matter-of-fact. "He'll be there, will he?"

"He'd better be," Daisy said. "Or the restaurant won't open tonight. Why?"

Nick shook his head. "Nothing, really. Just wondering."

"Has Toby said something to you?"

"About?"

"He's jealous..." Her face colored. "I mean don't make a big deal out of this, I'm not saying there's something going on that he should be jealous of—"

"Daisy. Just tell me."

"After you left my house, he called and started asking about you. I hung up on him."

"Does he always do this? With other men you're—"

She laughed. "There haven't been a whole lot of other men. Dating isn't really my thing." She shifted the bag to her other hand. "Toby's not violent. He's really just a big kid who never grew up. He makes these huge scenes when things don't go his way, but…" She shrugged. "It's just the way he is."

Nick nodded, not entirely convinced. Still, she had known Toby far longer than he had and, besides, it hardly seemed his business to appoint himself Daisy's bodyguard.

"Hey, I just thought of something. I'm having a hill-clearing party later this afternoon. I take the goats up to this spot above the canyon and everyone sits around sipping wine and eating cheese while the goats do their thing. It's a hoot. Want to come?"

"I'd love to."

CHAPTER FIFTEEN

"TONIGHT?" TOBY ASKED. The caller wanted to make reservations for a party of four. He tried not to laugh. "Sorry. No can do. We're booked solid."

He hung up the phone, which he shouldn't have to be answering because he was the executive chef, but Daisy was too damn cheap to spring for a part-time receptionist. He took another glance at the reservation book. Busy night. Like every night lately. Maybe he'd start a How Many People We Gonna Serve Tonight pool with the wait staff. They liked that sort of thing. It built morale.

From the refrigerator, he took a tray of filet mignon steaks and began to carve them into paper-thin slices for the carpaccio he'd put on the menu that night. Daisy would bitch about red meat again, but the hell with her.

He was a rising star in the culinary field.

He smiled to himself. Call him a perfectionist, okay, maybe he had a bit of an ego, too, but it was part of the business. Every plate that left his kitchen had to be perfect. Even a simple salad had to be just right.

Daisy with her damn cactus and all her other off-the-wall ideas.

She needed to just leave him the hell alone—well, except for the money. Truth was, everything about the restaurant business was cool. He couldn't even imagine doing anything else. A great chef could open a restaurant anywhere in the country, which he always reminded himself when Daisy started giving him a bad time.

It was hard work, though, no doubt about that. Long hours, attention to detail. You had to be in good shape, too. No one really understood that. Lifting heavy pots, being on your feet for eight hours, stirring vats of sauces, rolling pounds of dough. Last night Leah had told him he had a good body.

He grinned. He'd like to see Mr. Fancy Pants Biographer haul pots around. What really killed him was the way Daisy couldn't see the jerk was just a pretty boy. And not just Daisy, Emmy too. And Leah. *He's so cute.* Toby shook his head. Women really were nuts the way they couldn't see below the surface.

He'd worked up some pretty good steam about the guy by the time Daisy walked in. Right off, he could see she'd got this attitude about something. She hardly looked at him, just dumped this paper bag of lemons on the counter, put on an apron and started juicing the lemons.

"Nice to see you, too," he said.

"Cut it out, Toby, okay? I'm not in the mood."

She was standing with her back to him, sticking lemons on the juicer. He watched her for a minute. Her hair looked different, straight and shiny and nearly down to her waist. He never really thought much about how Daisy looked, she was just Daisy, but it suddenly hit him that she looked hot.

"So how's Nicky boy doing these days?" he asked. "Has he been by for another spot of tea?"

Nothing. She picked up the juice container, jiggled it around, checking the level, then started cutting up more lemons.

"Hey, I'm talking to you."

"I heard you."

"So quit ignoring me."

"Perhaps if you said anything remotely worth listening to…"

Toby's mouth dropped open. What? *Perhaps if you said anything remotely worth listening to.* "Oh and I guess Nicky is always worth listening to, huh? Mr. I Say Old Chap, may I have a spot of tea? I bet you never ignore him, huh?"

"Toby. Shut up."

"Don't tell me to shut up." He grabbed her arm and turned her so she had to look at him. Her eyes were huge. "Don't *ever* tell me to shut up, Daisy. You got that?"

"Let go of my arm," she said in this quiet voice. "Right now."

He tightened his grip so she'd know he meant business. "Maybe I don't write books and drive a damn Porsche, but I'm more man than he'll ever be, you got that?"

"I said let go of my arm."

"You puttin' out for him?" He squeezed harder. "Tell me Daisy, you giving him a little action?"

"Out." She jerked her arm free, moving so suddenly that he lost his balance and stumbled against her. Both hands on his chest, she pushed him away. "Get out. You're finished here."

He took a couple of breaths; he'd gone too far. "Look, I'm sorry—"

She grabbed his extra chef's jacket off the hook on the wall and shoved it at him. "And don't come back. You're fired."

He laughed. "Daisy come on, don't be crazy..." She had her arms folded across her chest. Her face looked all white and pinched, but she was madder than he'd ever seen her in all the years he'd known her. "I'm the damn chef, Daze. You can't fire me. I *am* Wildfire."

"Yeah? Well, I just extinguished your flames."

"Who's going to cook?"

"That's not your problem."

"Daisy, come on..."

She pointed a finger. "Go."

"You don't know what you're doing." He grabbed the jacket and started for the door. "I'm telling you Daze, you're gonna regret this."

NICK, IN THE best tradition of Hollywood movies, was walking along the waterline of the beach, talking on the mobile to his agent. His trousers were rolled up around his ankles, and his shirt flapped open in the breeze. But, like Truman's portrait of Daisy, the story behind the picture was less than idyllic.

"Nothing. Zippo. Zilch. Nada," Nick said.

Rod sighed.

"You think *you're* depressed? I've just financed a cottage in Devon on the strength of the advance for this book."

"Interested in something new?"

"Talk to me."

As his agent described the proposed project—a biography of a fairly minor Welsh politician, mostly a vanity piece that would have to be turned out quickly before the politico declared his candidacy for a higher office next year—Nick imagined himself back home, picking up the routine of his life in London. He would make an effort to see more of Bella, he would stop putting work first.

He would in all likelihood never see Daisy again.

"Look, hold off giving them an answer," he said. "Maybe I can reignite this Truman thing somehow."

"Glad to hear you say that," Rod said. "Frankly, I was surprised to see you give up quite so easily."

"I'm rather surprising myself these days."

"How so?"

"Oh…stray dogs. Washing dishes." He'd never been sentimental. Reason rather than emotion governed his behavior. If he loved A—to the point that he could love any woman—no reason why he couldn't also love B. Was there? Suddenly he was no longer so sure. "Just a general realization," he said vaguely.

"Right. Obviously more you're not telling me," Rod said. "But I'm not one to pry."

After he'd finished talking to Rod, he dialed his daughter's number.

"My God," he said when she actually answered the phone, "this is a first. I was ready to leave you a long-winded message. What time is it there? Shouldn't you be in bed?"

"I am in bed, Daddy. I've got a phone in my room, remember?"

"Ah. For all those late night calls, eh?"

"Mmm. Daddy? It's so horrible lately. Mummy has a boyfriend," she whispered. "And he's always over here. He has this hideous mustache that traps bits of food. I can't talk to him without looking at his mustache."

Nick grinned. "Why don't you just tell him about the crumbs? You'd probably be doing him a favor."

"I would if I could get a word in edgewise," Bella said. "But he never stops talking. I don't know how Mummy can put up with him."

Nick, still walking along the beach, had reached the steps that led up to the boardwalk that ran along the front of his apartment. He sat on the top step. "Do you have any holidays coming up? Because I was thinking…what about coming over here to stay with me for a while?"

IT WAS ONE THING to order Toby out of the restaurant, but quite another to deal with the consequences. Daisy glanced at the clock. One o'clock. The first reservation was for five. Damn it, why hadn't she paid more attention to what he did here every day?

The phone rang. It was Marla, one of the waitresses.

"Hey, Daisy. I've been sick to my stomach all morning. I'm not going to make it in tonight."

After Marla had hung up, the phone rang again almost immediately. Josh, the sous-chef. He'd gotten this bug that was going around. Couldn't get out of bed.

Down one waitress and one chef. Two chefs counting Toby. Well, she could wait tables if she had to. The two other waitresses could handle things. She walked over to the desk to check the specials. Salmon. Blackened steak with gingersnap dressing.

Gingersnap dressing? What the hell was gingersnap dressing? Where did Toby keep the recipes? She started flipping through his file drawer, pulling out folders. Nothing with recipes.

Leah would know. True, Leah had this thing with Toby now, but she'd worked at Wildfire since day one. She dialed the number and got Leah's answering machine.

"Leah, it's Daisy," she said. "I could really use your help. I…" She'd been about say that she'd told Toby to leave but decided against it. Leah might already have heard Toby's version, of course, but if not, no point in airing dirty laundry. "Anyway, we're going to be short-staffed tonight. Toby won't be here, Josh called in sick and so did one of the waitresses. Also, do you have any idea where Toby files his recipes? Please give me a call as soon as you get this, okay? Thanks."

She hung up the phone again. Any minute now, she would open her eyes, sit up in bed and realize that she'd been having a nightmare that the reservation book was full and she was standing there with no chef and no idea what they were going to serve that night.

Think. What would Toby usually be doing at this time? The truth was she had no idea. Usually she didn't arrive until three or so when she dropped off the desserts. Desserts. The lemons, some of them squeezed, were still on the counter partially juiced. She'd been tempted to pelt them at Toby's back.

The phone rang again. Please let it be Leah and let her know where the recipes are.

"Hey, Mom," Emily said.

"Hi, sweetie. What's up?"

"Kit wants to know if she needs to bring anything to the goat party."

The goat party. She'd forgotten the goat party. "Listen, something's come up at the restaurant and we're going to have to do the party another day."

"What happened?"

"Emmy…" She didn't want to get into the whole Toby thing right now. "Something came up and I'm going to have to cook tonight. Could you call Kit and—"

"Uncle Martin's here, that's the other reason I was calling. They're here to take me to some thing at this museum."

Daisy sighed. She could feel a headache coming on. "What thing at what museum?"

"You don't have to be so crabby," Emily said. "Hold on, Uncle Martin wants to talk to you."

Daisy groaned. "Hi, Martin."

"Emmy seemed surprised to see us. Did you forget to tell her we were coming? This was only planned—"

Daisy chewed her lip, debating whether or not to tell the truth. "Actually I forgot," she said, opting for the truth although she knew already it would set

Martin off on a lecture. She glanced at the time on her cell phone, predicted Martin would, if not stopped, go on for about ten minutes. "Martin, I don't have time for this, okay?"

"You sound agitated."

"I'm more than agitated. We've got a full house tonight and…" She was going to regret blurting this out, but she couldn't help it. "I had a fight with Toby and threw him out, so there's no chef tonight. The sous-chef and one of the waitresses called in sick, and I have no idea where to find any of Toby's recipes."

Martin laughed.

"It must be me," Daisy said, "but I'm just not seeing the humor."

"For God's sake, Daisy. You put yourself into these impossible situations, playing Mother Teresa to every deadbeat that sticks out a hand. What do you expect?"

"Thank you so much, Martin." *I'll have to remember this the next time I feel suicidal.* "Gotta go though."

"Oh, Daisy, don't take it all so seriously. Close the restaurant. Or buy some frozen pizzas and stick them in that fifteen-thousand-dollar brick oven."

Not a bad idea, Daisy thought, after she hung up. She could zip down to the market, load up on pizzas and call that the night's special. One day at a time, that was the key. She heard the front door open and, thinking it might be Toby coming back, she stuck her head out of kitchen.

"Nick!"

"I realized a couple of things after you left," he said. "One, I have no idea where the goat bash is taking place, and, two, what time does it start?"

"The goat party's been called off," she said.

"Oh." He seemed disappointed. "Goats off their food, or something?"

She shook her head. Nick was still standing just inside the front door. His shirt was unbuttoned and the khakis he wore were rolled up at the ankles and damp at the edges. He looked terrific. Not conventionally handsome, just windswept and dark-eyed and concerned and friendly, and it was all she could do not to just throw her arms around him and weep on his shoulder.

"I kicked Toby out," she said. "He had it coming. The problem is, we've got a full house tonight and half the restaurant staff has called in sick. My uncle suggested frozen pizza, and I was just thinking about running over to the market when you came in."

"Well, let's talk about it for a minute," Nick said. "Unless you're absolutely sold on the idea."

"No, not all." She motioned him inside. "Come on back."

"SHEPHERD'S PIE," Daisy said forty-five minutes later as she scrawled the night's special on a chalkboard. "Well, that's different, anyway." She glanced over at

Nick, shirtsleeves rolled above the elbows, whumping away at a huge pot of boiled potatoes. The smoked pork loin they'd shredded was simmering on the stove in an improvised gravy that, if she did say so herself, smelled fantastic. The shepherd's pie had been Nick's idea—his favorite childhood meal after baked macaroni and cheese, which was also on the menu along with a blackened steak salad and lots of roasted veggies. She didn't have time to deal with gingersnap gravy.

"You wouldn't really have to do much with the salmon, would you?" Nick looked up from his potato mashing. "Just grill it in the oven?"

She smiled. "Perfect. Ditto the chicken breasts."

"But they need a sauce, don't you think?"

Daisy fought to keep a straight face. Although he'd claimed he could hardly boil water, Nick was so clearly enjoying all this that she'd stopped thinking about dinner and a full house and no staff as a crisis and started having fun herself. He was describing a sauce that called for tarragon, but she was only half listening. The stereo in her head was playing "What Is This Thing Called Love?" and she was thinking that maybe it was like when you came down with the flu. Way before you're so sick, you can't even get out of bed, there's this virus doing its number on you, making you feel not quite yourself and wearing away at your defenses.

She was pretty sure she'd just succumbed.

SHE WAS EVEN MORE SURE as the evening wore on, and Nick calmly took on the combined roles of chef, waiter and general help as though he'd been pinch-hitting in restaurants his entire life. Before the first guests arrived, he'd assembled the partially baked shepherd's pies in small earthenware dishes usually used for French onion soup. "It's not exactly conventional, but then neither is smoked pork loin shepherd's pie. Still, no one's expecting English pub food."

The whole evening had been nonstop activity. As soon as one party left and the tables were cleared off, another was ready to be seated. It was like an intricate dance and they'd managed to keep step the whole time without exchanging more than a few words. Either she or Nick would come in from the dining room, sum up the situation and do whatever had to be done. While she was rescuing a curdled lemon sauce, for instance, and couldn't leave the kitchen to take in orders for a table of four, Nick had lined the plates down one arm and carried them into the dining room himself.

"You're amazing," she said, when the wave of diners had finally slowed to a trickle. He'd just set down a stack of dirty dishes and was leaning against the dishwasher taking a breather. A sudden image made her smile.

"What?"

"That first day I saw you here—"

"Oh, so long ago," he said, teasing her.

"It seems like ages. You were wearing a black linen jacket and your hair was in this neat little ponytail. You looked so sophisticated and European…"

He glanced down at himself. "You're suggesting that I no longer look European? Or sophisticated?"

She laughed. The chef's apron was a Rorschach test of gravy blobs and lemon sauce dabs and other unidentifiable things. His shirt cuffs, unbuttoned, had fallen about his wrists and although he'd rolled down his pants legs—remembering as he'd been on his way to the dining room—they were stained at the cuffs with salt water. He looked fantastic.

"We made quite a team, didn't we?" he said.

"I think so." Demurely, she smoothed the front of her apron. From the street, she could hear traffic and, faintly, the crash of the surf. More distinct was the hum and buzz and burr of appliances in the kitchen around them. "The only problem is—" she scratched at a dried blob on her apron "—I'll never be out of your debt."

He didn't say anything, and she rubbed away at the apron as though her life depended on it. When she glanced up, Nick was watching her and the tension was so tight she could have cut it with one of Toby's Japanese knives. It was the look on his face, the way her knees had gone all rubbery, the way all the air seemed sucked out of the room and then—she'd never be able to recreate how it happened, whether she moved forward or he did, or maybe they both moved together at the same time—Nick was holding her and she was up on her tiptoes to reach his mouth with hers, and they were kissing so hard she felt his teeth against her lip.

"Daisy." He turned her around so that her back was against the counter and kissed her again, pushing her back with his body until her shoulders were nearly horizontal and her head was hitting a stack of dirty dishes. "My God, Daisy," he said, when they finally broke away.

"I know." She held onto his shoulders, studied his face. His looked blurry somehow, dazed. Like hers, probably. What just happened already seemed impossible. That she had kissed her father's biographer, or he'd kissed her, while standing in the midst of a million dirty dishes in her ex-husband's restaurant. It was comic almost, like some far-fetched sitcom. And yet everything felt right, too.

"It's like you're just…Nick, and I've known you forever." The thought had popped into her head and, naturally, she'd had to give voice to it.

He smiled.

"About the goat party," she said. "I'm sorry you had to work instead."

"Mmm." He held her face between his hands and

kissed her softly on the mouth. "I would have enjoyed telling that story back in London."

"We could do it tomorrow," she said. "Except there won't be anyone else there, just you and me. And a herd of goats."

"I'll bring the wine and cheese."

"Damn," she said. "The dishes."

"Go home," he said. "I'll do them."

She looked at him. "Are you trying out for sainthood, or something?"

"Just trying to redeem myself for past sins."

THOSE WORDS CAME BACK to haunt him a couple of hours later when he returned to the apartment to find the place had been ransacked.

CHAPTER SIXTEEN

EVEN BEFORE HE TURNED on the light, Nick could see the mess. Papers were strewn all over the floor, the table he'd used as a desk was turned over on its side, clothes had been pulled from the closet. Food—orange juice, beer and eggs—had been removed from the fridge, then poured and broken over the scattered papers. His computer was gone, also a digital camera and about fifty dollars that he'd left lying on the bureau. The disk with his backup files was still under a pile of towels in the linen closet, which, given the amount of work he'd done recently was of little consolation.

He was almost certain he knew who did it, he told the policeman who responded to his call. Officer Ramirez didn't look particularly impressed one way or the other, but said the incident would be investigated.

"The man is a volatile, jealous lunatic," Nick said, anger finally replacing the zombie-like calm of disbelief he'd felt since he'd first unlocked the door.

"This—" he waved his arm to encompass the damage "—is because his ex-wife fired him and he obviously thinks—"

"You know that for a fact?"

"Well, no, but—"

"We'll look into it," the officer said.

"You don't believe me, do you? This isn't just a residential burglary, this is…" A thought occurred to him. "Has she ever taken out a restraining order against him?"

"I can't give you that information," the officer said. He made some notes as he took another look around. "Will you be staying here tonight?"

"What?" Nick thought for a moment. "No. I'm…I'll check into the Hotel Laguna, get a room for the night."

The officer gave him a business card with a number to call, told him they'd be in touch and left. Nick listened to the footsteps fade away on the wooden boardwalk below. If he needed a sign that this biography was doomed and had to be put out of its misery, this was about as subtle as a blow to the head.

He would bring Bella over for a few weeks, they'd do the California things. Disneyland, she'd already mentioned that, and all the other theme parks whose names she could rattle off as though she lived next door instead of a continent away. Maybe Daisy and her daughter would like to go along, too, although he rather imagined Daisy disapproving of that sort of thing. Exactly how he'd pay for the trip after he'd repaid the advance was another matter.

He yawned and glanced at his watch. He was still holding his keys. He closed the door behind him, not much point in locking really, walked down to the underground parking lot and got in the rented Toyota—quite a comedown from the Carrera but a necessary adjustment. Out on Pacific Coast Highway, he headed not for the Hotel Laguna but north toward Laguna Canyon Road. The wind was up, the palms in dark silhouette shaking like feather dusters. The air smelled of smoke and the chaparral and creosote bushes burning to the north and south…Daisy had told him about the chaparral. Last night as he'd parked in the underground garage, he'd found a thin layer of ash across the car's paintwork.

He slowed down as he approached the turnoff to Daisy's property. His first thought had been to take the dirt road all the way to the gravel footpath that led to her cabin, but he revised it as he drove.

While the idea of a sleepy Daisy answering his knock and taking him by the hand into her bedroom had enormous appeal, it was also problematic. No need to burden her with further evidence of Toby's instability. She'd sent him packing from the restaurant, obvious proof she'd had enough. The police had been called so there really wasn't much else to do.

All he wanted for the moment, he decided as his headlights picked up the bushes and shrubbery on either side of the dirt road, was to know that everything was okay inside Daisy's cabin. He knew Daisy's truck, which she usually parked beside the cabin, and he knew the rusted old warhorse Toby drove.

When he rounded the bend to her cabin, he saw only Daisy's vehicle. Breathing a sigh of relief, he headed a few yards back down the dirt road, pulled the car into the shrubbery, turned off the ignition and shifted the seat back as far as it would go. He then tipped his head back and resigned himself to waiting out the night. Too uncomfortable for sleep but not bad for a bit of overdue introspection.

A few hours later, with daylight creeping into the car, he righted the seat again. Creaky, cramped and in need of food and a shower, he started the ignition.

DAISY HAD JUST opened a box of sunflower seeds and was unlatching the door of the parrot's cage when Toby walked through the front door. None of the dogs had barked a warning. Toby was no threat, he'd walked through the door a hundred times before. Now the dogs milled around him, sniffing his shoes and vying for attention as he casually pulled out a chair and sat at the table.

Adrenaline coursing through her blood, Daisy tried to remember where she'd put the pepper spray.

Carefully, as though it were made of glass, she closed the door to the cage.

"Poor Deanna," the parrot said. "Who's a pretty girl?"

"Hey, Daze," Toby said brightly. Too brightly, though, like he was playing a part. His smile looked tight, wary, his body tensed. "What's up?"

Daisy's brain raced. He was wearing a faded blue-and-green checked shirt that she vaguely recalled buying for him years ago. Part of the collar was folded in at the nape of his neck as though maybe he'd dressed hurriedly to get over here. The radio had broken into regular programming to issue a red flag warning. ...*Ortega Hwy, Rancho Santa Margarita and Coto De Casa...fires widely separated, but winds increasing...firefighters from neighboring states...* "You wanna come out?" Deanna screeched. From Emmy's room, Daisy could hear the loud beat of loud music. Please don't come down.

"Toby, I want you to leave right now. Just leave. Let's not make this ugly. I don't want Emmy to—"

"How come? Lover boy's in the bedroom?"

"Listen, I've had it with making excuses for you. You need to grow up, pay your own bills, stand on your own two feet. You're talented, Toby, you'll find another job—"

"Crap." He brought his fist down on the table. Under the tan, his face had gone pale. "Where's all this coming from? Nicky Boy?" He got up from the table, started towards her. "Son-of-a-bi—"

"Get out, Toby." She pointed at the door. "Get out or I'm calling the police." She hadn't thought of doing that until just this moment, but the bruises on her left arm where he'd grabbed it yesterday were evidence if she needed it.

He glared at her. "You're asking for it, Daisy. Guess I'd better have a talk with Emmy. Tell her how, if you'd had your way, she wouldn't be around today."

"That threat won't work any more," she said. "I'm going to tell her myself."

"Daisy…" Suddenly, he just slumped, as though all the air had gone out of his body. He stuck his elbows on the table and held his head. "Daisy," he said again, his voice thick. "Please."

As she watched him, shoulders shaking, sobbing at the table, she felt her anger fade into sadness and re-sentment. He always did this, acted like a jerk and then played on her sympathies. And always, she'd relent.

He removed his hands from his face, gazed at her bleary eyes across the room. "I love you, Daze."

She shook her head. "No, you don't Toby, not…really. But it doesn't matter, anyway. I *don't* love you." She could hear her voice rising. This was no longer about what Toby wanted. This was about her life, and she suddenly felt what she was saying so intensely that her voice was shaking. "I'm sick of all this…I want a clean start. If you want the restaurant, you can buy out my half of it, but I want you out of my life."

Toby looked up then and she saw something change in his face, but she was so intent on making him understand how she felt that she kept talking about how she wanted her life to change. And then, with a big sigh, Toby stood.

"Okay, Daze," he said in a sad voice. "I don't know what to say to you. I did my best. That's all I know." He got up from the table, moving slowly as though his body was filled with lead and walked to the front door. "I love you, though." One hand on the doorknob, he shook his head. "I hope you know that. You and Emmy are my life." His voice cracked on the last word and then he was gone.

Daisy heard the screech of Emmy's voice, saw the white flash of movement and then, like a picture coming into focus, Emmy was standing there, fists clenched, long dark hair streaming around her shoulders.

"I hate you!" Emmy screamed. "You were so mean to Daddy." She stared at Daisy for a long moment and then ran, sobbing, into her room and slammed the door.

"Go away!" she screamed when Daisy knocked on her door a few minutes later. "I don't want to talk to you."

Daisy spent a couple of hours working off her anger, cleaning out the goat pen. Nothing like hurling around pitchforks of goat droppings to burn off pent-up feelings. She'd almost finished the work before she felt in control of her fury at Toby, who, obviously, had seen Emily in the doorway and amped up his dramatic performance for her benefit. She returned to the kitchen to find Emmy at the table, her face tear-splotched, eating toast and peanut butter.

"I'm sorry, Mom," she said without looking up. "I didn't mean it."

Breathless, her face still flushed from the exertion, Daisy sank onto the chair opposite Emmy. "I know you didn't, sweetheart." She scratched at a spot on the table. "Which isn't to say it doesn't hurt anyway…"

"I don't hate you," Emmy said, still addressing the piece of toast on her plate. "It's just that you seem, I don't know, strong. And Dad is like this little boy and I just feel sad for him."

"I feel sad for him, too," Daisy said truthfully. "But he's not a little boy and it doesn't help him, or anyone else, to keep making allowances for him."

"Mom." Emmy finally looked up. "Can you make some scrambled eggs?"

Daisy grinned. The world was back on its proper orbit. "I *can*…and so *can* you. Would you like me to make some?"

Emily nodded. "Mom, don't make some big deal out of this, okay?"

Daisy had just taken a carton of eggs from the fridge. She set them down on the counter and looked at Emily knowing, by her daughter's somber expression, that whatever she was about to hear was going to be a big deal regardless of what she promised. "Okay," she said, feigning a casual tone. "What's up?"

"I don't think Leah is good for Dad."

Daisy broke eggs into a bowl. "How come?"

"For one thing, all the vegetables she uses are canned, but that's not it." She paused. "I think she and Dad are, like, tweaking or something."

Daisy turned to look at her. "You mean using drugs?"

Emily nodded. "When I was over at Leah's for dinner…" She shook her head. "Just the way they were acting. And, like, Leah's real, real thin."

Daisy looked at the yellow yolks floating in the blue bowl on the counter. She'd just picked up a fork to break them, but she'd suddenly lost her appetite. She sat at the table opposite Emmy and stared at her daughter.

"I don't want you to go to Leah's apartment again, okay?"

"Mom…I said don't make a big deal."

"Drugs *are* a big deal." She thought of the bruises under the sleeve of her shirt, debated showing them to Emmy. She decided not to; she didn't know whether Toby had been using drugs when he grabbed her. *I'm going to talk to your father*, she started to say but stopped herself. She was not Toby's guardian. If he was using drugs, she would go to court to keep him from seeing Emmy, but she wouldn't burden Emmy with that right now.

"I'm not going to go shooting myself up, if that's what you're thinking," Emily said when the silence had stretched on for a while. She grinned at Daisy. "Come on, Mom. You're not responsible for the whole world."

Daisy sighed. She felt as drained as if someone had just squeezed her around the middle and wrung out every bit of energy. Last night Nick had just taken over at the restaurant—cooked, cleaned, waited on tables—and it had been okay. Or maybe it wasn't that he'd taken over as much as they'd formed a working partnership. Maybe she *wasn't* responsible for the whole world, but she felt as though she were. And she didn't like the feeling. She wanted to tell Nick the one thing she hadn't told him about her father; she wanted it all out there. Maybe he'd see her in a different way after that, but it didn't matter… Well, it did. She wanted him to go on looking at her the way he had last night, but she had to take the risk anyway.

"…and that thing Dad said about the abortion," Emmy was saying.

Daisy snapped to attention. "What?"

"That you wanted to have an abortion? I already knew that. Dad told me ages ago. It's, like—" she flicked the hair back from her face "—like the me I am now isn't the same as…okay, what am I trying to say?" A smile twitched at the corners of her mouth, spread into a full-on smile. "It's like how would you know I was going to turn into this great kid? You couldn't, right?"

Someone knocked at the door and Emily jumped up.

"Hey Nick," she said. "How's it going? Wow, awesome flowers."

DAISY HAD THE slightly distracted air of someone interrupted. She wore jeans ripped at the knees and the Doesn't Play Well With Others T-shirt.

He nodded his head at her chest. "Should I take this as a warning?"

"Huh?" Realization dawned. "Hold on, I'll get the one that says, I Didn't Order This Day.'"

"See you, Nick," Emily squeezed past him but not in time to avoid Daisy's outstretched hand. "What?"

"Where are you going?"

"Over to Kelsey's. Remember? We have tennis practice?"

"Where's your racket?"

Emily sighed as though even the scant supply of

patience she'd been able to hold on to was finally exhausted. "Mom. It's at Kelsey's."

"Emily, my daughter's coming out here for a visit," Nick said, realizing, too late, that it might have been better to mention it to Daisy first, instead of blurting it out. He'd just been on the phone with Bella before he left, though, and it was on his mind. "Next week. I hope you'll be able to show her around."

"Cool. No problem." She looked at her mother. "So, can I go now? Please?"

Daisy still looked as though her mind was elsewhere. "Okay, but remember what I said—"

"I *know*, Mom." She smiled. "Bye, you guys."

After Emily left, Daisy looked down at the flowers as though she'd suddenly realized they were there. "These are gorgeous. I'm sorry, I…"

He watched as she stuck her head into the bouquet—a rainbow of exotic blooms, none of which he could name, although he recalled the florist mentioning tiger lilies and heliotrope.

"Thank you," she said, finally coming up for air. "Why, though?"

He laughed. "Is that your usual response when a chap buys you flowers?"

Her face colored. "Chaps don't often buy me flowers. Not that I'm feeling sorry for myself, or anything …"

He caught her face in his hands. "Hello, Daisy."

"Hi, Nick." She smiled. "I should be buying you flowers."

He kissed her and, still holding the flowers, she put her arms around him and buried her face in his shirtfront.

"How long did you stay washing dishes last night?" she asked.

"Not long." He felt damp through his shirt and pulled away slightly to look at her. Her eyes were wet. He thought immediately of Toby—whom he wouldn't be surprised to see turning up any moment. "Let's go somewhere," he said. His apartment was out of the question, another police officer had been by just before he left. No indication they were taking his claim seriously although they had asked him for Toby's phone number. "Where is it you take the goats?"

"The goats?" Her hands shot to her mouth. "Oh, damn, the goat thing. Listen…oh, and I need to put the flowers in water. I think I'm going crazy. Thank God today's Monday," she said as she walked into the kitchen.

"Because…"

"Because…" She was on her hands and knees digging through a cabinet. "I know I have a vase here somewhere…because the restaurant's closed Monday, but after today, who knows? Toby came by earlier…"

Her voice trailed off so he didn't know what had transpired with Toby. He took the flowers from the sink and stuck them in an empty peanut butter jar, also in the sink. Daisy was still mumbling about a vase and opening cabinet doors. He took her by the shoulders, turned her around toward the door and walked her in the direction of the car, Daisy chattering all the while about things she'd remembered that she needed to do. "Forget everything, all right?" he said. "Just climb aboard my magic carpet and let me whisk you away from all this."

THE MAGIC CARPET made its first, unscheduled, stop less than ten minutes later halfway down Laguna Canyon Road.

"Nick." Daisy grabbed his arm. "Stop. Right now. Please."

With no idea why, he steered to the side of the road. In an instant, Daisy was out of the car and, barely stopping to look at oncoming traffic, had darted around to look at something close to the car's right front tire. He got out himself and found her gently probing the body of what looked like a rabbit.

"He's dead,' she said. "You didn't hit him, he's cold. He was dead already. They don't stand much chance against two-ton trucks."

Nick looked at her, at a loss for words. How many dead animals had he seen on the roadsides of different countries? In Australia, he'd seen three dead kangaroos before he'd even set eyes on a live one. Small dead creatures, some mangled beyond recognition—he'd hardly given them a second thought.

Daisy was sitting on the grass, tears dropping onto her lap. "I need to bury it," she said. "I always keep a shovel in the truck." She sighed, a long, shuddering intake of breath. "Once I counted five, just on Laguna Canyon Road."

"And you stopped to bury every one of them."

She nodded. "They deserve at least that."

Sitting there on the side of the road with Daisy and the dead rabbit and cars whizzing by, Nick had a sudden memory of Chairman Meow and his own cynical musings at the burial of that animal. He doubted the man he'd been then would have had much patience with Daisy. But then Daisy had been the instrument of his change. He put his arm around her and she cried on his shoulder.

"I know," she said after a while. "I'm hopelessly weird."

"Are you crying for this rabbit?" Nick asked. "Or dead animals in general?

"I don't know." She sniffed and wiped her eyes. "Everything, I think. All the things, the people, I've tried to help and it just hasn't worked out...I feel awful."

"Have you ever thought that you're a bit too hard on yourself?"

She shook her head. "No." A moment or two passed, and then she said, "I left out the most important part when I told you about my father the other night. I killed him, Nick. I killed my dad."

CHAPTER SEVENTEEN

FOR A MOMENT NEITHER of them spoke. Daisy sat with her head bowed. The sun had gone down and the air was starting to cool.

"I can't believe I actually said those words," she finally said. "They've been in my head for so long. They've haunted my dreams…and now they're out there." She turned her head to look at him. "I did say them, didn't I? It wasn't just my imagination?"

Nick had his arm around her shoulders still, but she was shivering violently. Her face, illuminated in a passing headlight, was distraught and wild-eyed. Without a word, he pulled her to her feet, then carried the rabbit to the far edge of the grass verge, covered it with leaves and twigs, and got Daisy into the car.

They ended up at a small, dark bar, down near the harbor in Dana Point. The booths were cracked red vinyl, and amber candles burned in plastic mesh-covered holders, but it was comfortable and quiet and after Daisy had finished a coffee laced with brandy, she stopped shivering.

"Do you want me to tell you the rest?"

"If you want to tell me," he said.

"That night, the night he died, we'd had this horrible fight. I'd been staying away from the house more and more. I just couldn't stand to be there. Everything he did irritated me or hurt my feelings." She cradled her hands around the empty coffee cup. "He'd always complain that he was lonely, that he missed me, but the things he did, the way he behaved…he was belligerent and aggressive, brushing off anything I said or getting angry. I'd sometimes wonder if he was *trying* to drive me away."

The front door swung open and two middle-aged women walked in on a wave of noise from the highway. One of them glanced over at Daisy. He thought for a moment it was someone she knew, but after conferring for a moment, heads close, the women made their way to the far end of the room and sat down on stools at the bar.

Daisy took a breath. "I'd told him I was pregnant, that's what the fight was about. He'd been in bed reading. It was early, five-thirty or so, but he had a cold. It was early November so it was already dark outside, and the wind was blowing, but it was warm so the windows were open." She shrugged. "He slept with them open even when it was cold outside."

She stared down blankly at the beat-up table. "He was lying in his big bed, the head of it up against the window. He was telling me I'd ruined my life, ruined his, too, that I was stupid and careless and trying to hurt him." She traced her finger around the rim of the mug. "There wasn't anything my father couldn't somehow relate to himself."

Nick had his arm around her shoulder, but he felt as if she were a million miles away.

"A candle was burning on the table by the bed," she said. "He'd light them most evenings, then have a few drinks and fall asleep. 'You're going to burn the house down one day,' I used to tell him." She laughed bitterly. "I remember looking at the candle flickering in the breeze from the window. I remember seeing the edge of the curtain blowing close to the flame, but I didn't say anything."

She rubbed her eyes, then drew a long breath. "Toby was waiting downstairs. I was crying. I told him my dad had kicked me out…"

"Daisy." Nick pulled her closer. Tears were streaming down her face. "You don't have to do this—"

"No, no." She shook her head. "I want to. I *have* to." She gulped down half a glass of water. "Toby promised he would take care of me, and I was scared and lonely and I went with him. He was driving fast, I remember, whipping around corners. I told him to slow down. When we got down to Coast Highway, the traffic was bumper to bumper and you could smell smoke. A new wildfire was burning in one of the canyons. I could hear sirens off in the distance. We were heading north, Toby lived in Santa Ana, but the traffic was hardly moving. I don't know why, but I turned to look back into the hills—you could see my father's house, the bedroom windows along the second floor. My father's room was the one on the end. It was glowing bright orange."

"HOW COME YOU'RE getting mad at me?" Emmy was lying on the couch watching TV. "It's not my fault what you guys do."

"I know, hon, I know." Toby paced the living room of his apartment. One reason he was getting mad at her was that she'd caught a ride over and just showed up on his doorstep when he wasn't expecting her. The other reason was she'd just given him a lecture on doing drugs. Pretends she's just stopped by to see him, then starts nagging him about how drugs were bad and laying this guilt trip on him. So he was mad at her and mad at himself, because it was pretty pathetic when your teenage kid had to lecture you on drugs. And then thirty minutes after she gets there, she wants him to take her home again.

And then she has to tell him about Nick bringing Daisy a fancy bunch of flowers that probably cost more than he made in a month except that now he wouldn't be making squat in a month because he didn't have a job. Who wouldn't be mad? The only good thing was that there was this computer at the back of his closet that had to have cost some bucks, which was why he needed to go talk to this guy he knew. Another reason he wasn't exactly thrilled when Emily just showed up. Still he couldn't help wondering what Mr. Big Bucks had thought when he'd got back to his little bachelor pad.

"So just tell me about it again," he asked Emmy. "Mr. Hot Shot? He didn't say anything?"

She was channel surfing, bored. "About what?"

"I don't know, about anything."

She laughed. "Well, jeez Dad, if you don't know what you mean, how am I supposed to? I'm not a mind reader, you know."

"'I'm not a mind reader, you know,'" he said making fun of her because he didn't like her smart-ass attitude.

"If you're going to be hateful, why don't you just take me home?"

"Because I've got somewhere else I need to be."

"Fine." She flipped through the channels some more. "And you shouldn't call Nick 'Mr. Hot Shot.' He's nice. I like him."

Okay, that did it. Like he didn't have enough on his mind. First Daisy, now his daughter. And who ends up getting screwed? Yours truly, thank you very much.

He took his jacket off the back of the chair and started for the door. "Back in a few."

"Where're you going?"

"We need milk."

"There's a whole half gallon in the fridge."

"Eggs then." He slammed the door behind him before she could make a federal case of it just like her mother was always doing. Down in the courtyard, he smoked a quick joint around the back of the Dumpsters, keeping an eye out for the cops. He could smell the rotten vegetables. He'd done so much stuff, weed alone wasn't enough lately, Daisy could thank herself for that, with the way she'd been throwing herself at that guy.

She was going to pay for it too; they both were. Daisy was going to learn her lesson soon enough. Once she told Nick all he wanted to know, the bastard would be off quicker than you could say *jet plane*. He felt bad for Daisy because, go figure, he still loved her even if she was making his life hell. He didn't feel bad for Mr. Biographer though. That jerk deserved everything he had coming and more.

CHAPTER EIGHTEEN

"…AND I DON'T want to make him sound like some kind of monster," Daisy said. "He was so sweet sometimes. He could be touched by the smallest, insignificant things. Things most people wouldn't even notice. He'd pick up a sneaker left on a sidewalk, a carnation that must have fallen out of a bouquet, and he'd have this incredibly tender expression…."

Nick glanced at her, at the play of firelight across her face. They were sitting on the floor of her cabin, in front of the fire, on either side of the low coffee table where Daisy had set the omelets she'd made for them. She held her wineglass between both hands, as though drawing warmth from it. Her omelet was untouched.

"One time we were in Dublin on St. Patrick's Day," she said. "We'd just seen the parade where everyone waved these green and orange plastic flags. Afterward, people were walking over the flags that had just been tossed away. My dad bent down and picked one up." She smiled. "He gently smoothed it out, like it was sad to see it all trampled."

The night her father died, she'd left Toby, stuck in traffic north of town and ran back to the house, a thirty-five-minute uphill jog. She'd arrived minutes ahead of the fire engines to find her father's house and the two adjacent houses in flames.

"My father died because I was angry at him," she'd told him at the bar. "Too angry to be bothered to blow out the damn candle."

Now, she reached across the table to grab his wrist. "Nick. Where are you?"

He smiled. "Right here with you."

"You look a long way away."

"You didn't eat your omelet."

"I know. I thought I was hungry, but I guess I wasn't. Want it?"

He shook his head. "Not that it wasn't good."

"How do you feel about doing the biography now?" she asked.

He took a sip of wine, set the glass down again. "I don't know," he replied truthfully. Daisy's story had given the whole thing a very different perspective, but he couldn't imagine separating out his personal feelings for her to approach the book with anything close to objectivity about her father. The genesis of the project, the impression he'd had of a father's love reflected in the portrait of his daughter, was no longer viable. There were two very different sides to Frank Truman. He understood that now and he doubted he could portray the dark side without hurting Daisy.

He leaned his head against the back of the couch, closed his eyes, then felt Daisy's face next to his.

"Boo," she said.

He pulled her close and kissed her hard on the mouth. Without breaking contact, she slid beneath him and soon they were sprawled half off the couch, her skirt up around her thighs.

"Where's Emily?" he said, his lips against her neck.

"At Kelsey's, but I don't know if she's staying the night…"

And then, as though Emily had actually walked into the room, they simultaneously sat up like children caught in the act of mischief. Daisy adjusted her clothes, patted her hair. He picked up a cushion that had been knocked to the floor, set it back on the couch. Daisy grinned at him and he laughed and kissed her again.

"You…" He shook his head, words eluding him.

She was still smiling. "You, too…"

"Can I say something, Daisy?"

"No." She shook her head. "Whatever you have to say, I don't want to hear it. Just be here."

"You did not kill your father."

"Nick, no."

"I'm sorry, I have to. Someone should have set you straight years ago. He was a grown man, Daisy. A brilliant artist. He chose to have a candle burning. It's ludicrous, the idea of you taking on the responsibility, beating yourself up over it for all these years."

She put her fingers over his lips. "Nick. Thank you."

He took her hand. "I'm serious—"

"I know you are, and I appreciate it. But you *weren't* there. I'd like to feel…absolved of it, but you saying it doesn't make it so. I *could* have snuffed out the candle and I didn't." She caught his hand, held it between her own.

"The thing is, now I've told you all this, it feels like such a burden is gone. It's as if I've created this image of my dad that has grown bigger and bigger over the years. Getting it out in the open brings it down to size. I *want* you to write the book, Nick. I want you to write it as much now as I didn't want you to write it before."

He laughed. The green digital readout on the stereo flashed over to 11:48. "Let's talk about it tomorrow." But another thought occurred to him as they stood at the front door. "Let's not talk about it tomorrow, maybe not for several days. Let's just let things settle down a bit and—" he put his arms around her "—let's go to the Hotel Laguna tomorrow."

She grinned. "Oka-a-y," she said slowly. "And…"

"Let's pretend we're Bogie and Bacall."

"BE VERY CAREFUL," the old crone in Daisy's dream warned. "Be very, very careful."

Daisy sat up in bed, sweating. She felt strange, not sick but not quite well. As though she'd come through this serious illness and was just now beginning to feel like herself again but not entirely. Still half-asleep, she realized that what she thought was the old crone's voice was the phone ringing. She grabbed the receiver just as the message machine started to kick in.

"Hi," she said. "Hold on." She heard her voice and the click and the whirr of the machine and then Nick's voice.

"…and I've been awake all night," he was saying. "So, if I don't seem to be making much sense to you, then you can put it down, in part, to sleep deprivation, but it's not entirely that…Bella's mother was in an accident last night, the car she was driving was broadsided. She'll pull through, but Bella is distraught and frightened—"

"Oh, my God, Nick." Daisy, wide awake now, sat up in bed. "That's awful. Is there something I can do? Anything—"

"Thank you." There was a beat of silence. "You're incredibly kind. I've, uh, well the fact is I've been sort of moving in and out of people's lives for far too long and I'm not very happy with myself as a person and…"

Daisy felt her breath catch. He was saying something else, but she was still caught up on *incredibly kind*. What sort of thing was that to say to someone you were supposed to be playing Bogie and Bacall with in just a few hours? A cold lump had formed somewhere in her chest; her hands had tightened into claws around the receiver. She took a breath. "Nick, back up a second." But he went on talking about Bella and going back to England as though he hadn't heard her.

"I'm trying to book a flight back and, the thing is, Daisy, I'm going to have to abandon this project. I haven't exactly set the biographical world on fire to date, but I do take a certain amount of—"

"Wait." Her heart was hammering now, the cold lump replaced by a bongo drum. "By *this project* you mean the biography of my father?"

"Yes. Right. Sorry if it came off the wrong way, I—"

"*You're sorry.*" She was almost hyperventilating, and she took a few breaths to calm down. "You know what? I want to just slam the phone down on you, but I'm not going to because there are too damn many questions I need you to answer." She got out of bed and, phone in hand, started walking around the room, then down the hall into the kitchen. The dogs had been sleeping, but now they followed her, their toenails clicking like a castanet band. In the kitchen, she leaned against the counter. The parrot was hanging upside down from her perch. "I don't even know where to start…but wait, maybe I'm jumping to conclusions. You didn't really intend to just casually tell me over the phone that you're *abandoning* this project? Please tell me that—"

"Daisy, what can I say? I was intrigued by the idea of writing your father's story. You, of course, were an added dimension. But then the whole thing became hopelessly muddled."

"*Muddled.*" She'd turned into a parrot herself. "What's muddled supposed to mean?"

"I lost my focus," Nick said. "It happens sometimes. The trick is knowing when to call it quits."

Daisy slammed down the receiver. She couldn't stand to listen to any more of it. *But what about us?* she'd wanted to ask, except that it sounded too pathetic. Obviously she'd been wrong; there was no "us." For a few moments, the room actually seemed to spin around.

I can't believe this, I cannot believe this.

"Poor Deanna," the parrot said. "Poor, poor Deanna."

"Aw, shut up," Daisy said.

The phone rang again.

She stared at it. Counted to five and grabbed the receiver. "You're calling to say you don't know what came over you?"

"Huh?" Toby said. "Daisy?"

Daisy closed her eyes. *Please, I don't need this now.*

"I was gonna bring Emmy home and I thought maybe we could talk if you had some time."

"Emmy." Something broke through the fog. "Emmy is with Kelsey."

Toby laughed. "Jeez, I could have sworn she was sitting right here in front of me. Maybe you'd better start paying more attention to your daughter instead of smooching it up with Nick."

"Get her home right now," Daisy said. "And forget the talk. I have nothing to say."

She slammed down the receiver again. This could become habit-forming, she thought.

Later that morning Martin called.

"No, I don't know why he changed his mind," she told him. "What did he tell you? Yeah, well that's what he told me, too. Some projects work out, some don't. How does it feel being a project anyway? No, I'm not taking it personally, I'm just…why would I be crying? I've got things on my mind."

She hung up as fast as she could. Of course she was taking it personally. Of course she was crying. Martin was talking about Nicholas Wynne, the biographer. She was talking about Nick, the guy who'd held her on the beach, who'd kissed her in the firelight. She blew her nose. Tears streamed down her face. She picked up the blender, thought about throwing it. She set it down. On her bedside table, if she were to go in there, she would find Baba's book. But Baba would say something about detachment which was too late for her. She'd been attached. Now she was detached and it hurt.

Amalia called just after noon.

"What is this with Nicholas, Daisy? Why did he change his mind? What did you tell him?"

She had no answers for Amalia. What *do* you say to a guy you've known for all of two weeks when he says, as any reasonable person could guess he would end up saying, that he's going back where he came from?

See you. Nice talking to you. Don't let the door hit you on the way out.

She could only speak for herself but she was going to demand a little more of an explanation. And since Mr. Nicholas Wynne had apparently decided to stop taking phone calls—she'd left four messages since he called that morning, quite a change from the days when she'd stopped even counting his phone messages to her—she would have to go to him.

She drove down to the village, feeling only slightly guilty as she passed Wildfire and the chalked message board that read, Closed Until Further Notice. She parked on the street outside Nick's apartment. Was it weird that she'd never been inside? Maybe, except that maybe it was also further proof of how little she really knew about him. Maybe his name wasn't even Nick. Maybe, he was a modern day Jack the Ripper and she'd got out just in time.

Every thought has a consequence. Okay, Baba, she'd try to remember that.

Reining in her fantasies, she knocked on the door. No answer.

She knocked again.

"Are you looking for Nick?" A blonde in a sprayed-on denim shirt and gigantic silver hoop earrings poked her head out from the next balcony. "He's not in."

"I was coming to that conclusion," Daisy said.

"He hasn't been staying there since his apartment got broken into."

Daisy did a double take. "I'm sorry?"

"His apartment was broken into. About two days ago. His computer and everything was taken, the whole place was totally ransacked."

Two days ago would have been…she tried to think. The night he worked at Wildfire. The same night she fired Toby. Kaleidoscopic pieces were tumbling over in her brain, forming new and disturbing pictures. "Do you know where he is now?"

"No idea," the blonde said. "You want me to give him a message if I see him?"

"Yeah," Daisy said, and then changed her mind. "No, forget it. Thanks anyway."

She drove to the police station. Yes, the officer on duty confirmed, a break-in had been reported. Other than that, they were spectacularly unhelpful. Ditto Toby. She'd found him at his apartment in Santa Ana, on his very best behavior but wounded that she would even suspect him of doing anything like that.

"What really kills me, Daze," he said, "is that you don't even know this guy. He just comes out of the woodwork, all charm and big talk, but right away you'd take his side. You don't even know what enemies he has, could be anyone. Some jealous husband, an ex-girlfriend—"

"Toby, he lives in England. He's only been in town a couple of weeks."

"He's a fast mover, what can I say?"

Toby had a point there, she had to admit.

"YOU FILL UP MY senses," John Denver was singing on the radio in the kitchen, "like a light in the forest."

"God, who believes that stuff?" Her eyes streaming, she snapped off the radio. Somehow she was busily making another Wacky cake with no idea of how she'd reached the decision to make one and no recollection even of getting things out of the pantry. She didn't even want Wacky cake. It was so strange, to find that the things you turned to for comfort had suddenly stopped working.

It had been twenty-four hours since she'd heard from Nick, and she couldn't pretend it didn't hurt. She also couldn't deny that she'd entertained fantasies of him declaring his undying love for her. Even though she'd never really moved beyond that point, the idea of being in love with Nick, of having it reciprocated, had filled a part of her that now felt empty and cold.

There *were* positives. The way they'd sat on the side of the road, the night she'd told him about how her father died. She could still feel the weight of his arm around her shoulder, see the way passing cars had slowed down after spotting them there, the way Nick had waved them on.

I must stop thinking about this. He's going back to England. To Valerie and Chairman Meow, well, no, Chairman Meow is dead. So sad, poor cat. Fine one minute, dead the next. She started crying again. Nick, by his own admission, had not liked Chairman Meow though which, right then, should have tipped her off about his true character.

I mustn't think about anything. I must make my mind completely blank.

Craving distraction that didn't involve food, she seized on the mail the minute Emmy brought it in. Emmy gave her a look; usually the mail sat ignored on the table after Daisy flipped through it quickly to see whether there was anything that needed her immediate attention. A pale violet envelope caught her eye, mostly because it smelled like the cheap perfume Toby used to buy her after he'd been cheating on her. The return address was a post office box in Dana Point. The name above it read Audrey Myerson. The envelope was so thin she could almost read the writing on the letter inside.

She ripped it open.

Dear Daisy,

I have some information regarding your father that I would like to share with you. I'm contacting you about it at this time because I understand a Mr. Nicholas Wynne is planning a biography. I don't know how you feel about that, but in any case I have some information about your father that you might want to hear about. Please call me at the above number.

Daisy stared at the letter for a long time, then she picked up the phone and called Audrey Myerson.

CHAPTER NINETEEN

"I HOPE YOU'RE not expecting *me* to feel sorry for *you*," Valerie said over the phone from her dreary flat in dreary London. "You didn't honestly expect her to greet you with open arms after all this time."

Daisy or Bella? Nick almost said, except that he knew she meant Bella. He'd been ready to go immediately back to England to be with her after Avril's accident, had purchased the tickets in fact, when Bella rang him to say she was quite all right with her Auntie Helen, who had two enormous black cats and a really big back garden with lots of toys. It was probably better for her to stay there, she'd said, since Nick's London flat was so small, and there was really nothing for her to do there anyway. She still wanted to come to California, she'd assured him. "But not till Mummy is completely better."

He'd taken an apartment south of Laguna, less expensive, bought another computer and accepted several short-term assignments for financial reasons and to occupy his mind while he tried to sort out his thoughts about Daisy. Contrary to what he'd told her, he hadn't entirely abandoned the biography. but its prognosis was hour-to-hour, largely depending on how inspired and optimistic he happened to be.

Reviving it would mean earning her forgiveness, and his chances in that regard seemed as glum as he was feeling. He was deliberately not checking his messages back at the Laguna apartment until he'd reached some firm decisions. Meanwhile Daisy haunted his dreams, filling his head and generally making him feel more miserable than he'd ever imagined he could feel over a woman.

"In the child's entire life, when have you ever really been there for her?" Valerie asked him. "And now just because you've hit a low spot, you expect her to be there for you."

"Rubbish," Nick said. "First of all, I have not hit a low spot, as you put it."

"No? How's the definitive biography coming along?"

"Well, that..."

"And the ransacked apartment?"

"That, too."

"And Gillian mentioned a woman."

"Gillian should be gagged."

"Did she give you the boot?"

"Gillian?"

"This woman. Gill said the night you met her for

drinks, you were rather mysterious about it, but she had the distinct impression that you'd met someone. You can tell me, Nick, it's quite all right. I won't be the least bit jealous. *I* have someone in *my* life. Not that you asked, but things are going very well with Richard."

"Glad to hear it," Nick said. He was. Which wasn't to say he wouldn't welcome a few things going well for him. He'd gone back to his ransacked apartment after leaving Daisy, and suddenly the whole bloody mess had seemed like a metaphor for his own life. Not only was he disgusted with it himself, the idea of involving Daisy in it any further struck him as too incredibly selfish. Even Toby's carnage seemed somehow brought on by his own arrogance. The Porsche, the oceanfront apartment. And then blithely assuming Toby's role at the restaurant and, for an elegant finishing touch, making romantic overtures to the man's ex-wife over a stack of dirty dishes. Whether or not Toby knew any of that, he'd obviously sensed something.

"Well, what about this woman?" Valerie, who'd been yammering on about what a perfect love Richard was wanted to know. "Are you besotted?"

Nick grinned, despite his generally bleak mood. "Besotted?" *Made confused through affection or attraction to someone.* "Yes, I think I probably am."

"And what are you going to do about it?"

"Don't know," he said. "That's why the term is apt."

"What exactly is it that confuses you?"

"About Daisy? Nothing, really. She has this habit of saying whatever's on her mind." He smiled again. "It's disconcerting and endearing. She's a bit quirky, but very tenderhearted. We were driving and she saw this dead rabbit…?

"Ugh."

"Yes, well, Daisy didn't quite see it that way. She wanted to bury it."

"*Why?*"

"Oh, it's a long story. I handled the whole thing rather poorly."

"The rabbit, you mean?"

"The way things were left between us."

"What did you do?"

"Essentially, I ran."

"Essentially, what you've always done," she said.

"Essentially, yes. But I'm ready to take a different approach."

"About time, I should say."

IT TOOK DAISY LESS than ten minutes to figure out that she didn't like Audrey Myerson, and not much longer to figure out that Audrey was her mother. They were sitting on the patio of a Dana Point restaurant overlooking the harbor and Audrey was complaining that the "cigarette Nazis" had gone too far when they'd banned smoking at outside tables and she wished to hell people would mind their own business and get on with their own miserable lives instead of sticking their noses in hers.

"Yeah, what's a little secondhand smoke?" Daisy asked. She couldn't stop herself. Looking at Audrey was like looking at herself twenty-five years or so down the road—red hair faded to gray, but still coarse and wavy, freckles…Audrey's were mixed in with a spattering of age spots, and her skin was parched and sagging around the jowls. Except for the brief moment that Audrey had lowered her sunglasses when they'd first met, her eyes had been hidden, but Daisy had caught a quick glimpse of cat-green irises, bloodshot whites.

Audrey had ordered a Jack Daniel's, downed it and, while Daisy was still drinking iced tea, motioned to the waiter for another. As soon as they'd sat down, she'd launched into stories about Frank. Most of the stories Daisy had already heard, but it wouldn't have mattered, she could barely listen to this woman for wanting to blurt out, *You're my mother*.

It seemed so incredible. She wanted to peel back the woman's skin, unlatch the top of Audrey Myerson's head and peer inside. What was going on in there? *Do you know I know who you are?* But how could she not?

"You got kids?" Audrey filled in a gap in her monologue to ask.

Okay, this was it. Daisy wanted to tell Audrey to take off her sunglasses. She wanted to look the woman in the eyes as she told her she was a grandmother.

"Yeah." She nodded, but if Audrey was sending out the tiniest shreds of grandmotherly vibes, they were undetectable. "I have a daughter, Emily. She's fourteen." She reached for her bag. "Want to see a picture?"

Audrey shrugged. "Sure. Why not?" When Daisy handed her Emmy's latest school picture—braces, hair pulled back into a tight knot that emphasized her green eyes and sharp cheekbones—Audrey held it at arm's length and lifted her sunglasses to squint at it.

"Who does she look like?"

"She's got my eyes." She looked directly at Audrey. *And yours.* "And she freckles like me, but she's got her father's dark hair."

"Toby."

Daisy nodded, suddenly aware of her breathing.

"I was with Frank the night you told him you were pregnant."

"The night he died," Daisy said.

"We'd been seeing each other on and off for years…until I got pregnant. Wasn't easy to hide it from Amelia—"

"Amelia." She drank some water, set the glass down. "So my dad was cheating on her…with you?"

"Your dad cheated on any woman he could find, honey."

Daisy felt her bottom lip quiver. She was not going to cry in front of this woman. Deep breaths. Forgiveness. Heart opening like a flower. She drank some more water.

"Amelia catches us one day and clears off to Portugal. Of course, your father blames me for everything. Nothing was ever his fault. Ever. I shouldn't have been at the cottage—even though he'd brought me down there in the first place. Then, just like that, it was all over, he was through with me. I gave up the baby, thought about having an abortion, but Frank talked me out of it." She downed half her drink, patted her mouth with a paper napkin. "You've probably figured things out, huh?"

"I was the abortion you thought about having?"

Audrey flinched. "I was a model, lingerie shots, nothing sleazy. You know, the department store ads that come in the newspaper, that sort of thing. Nine months of pregnancy would have meant nine months of no income."

Daisy couldn't take her eyes off Audrey's face. It seemed as though the whole world had narrowed down to this patio and this table. Her existence had been a toss-up. Her mother, *her mother*, was casually acknowledging that she'd had to choose between a baby or a modeling career. She wanted to go and find Emmy and just hold her forever. *You didn't know what a great kid I would turn out to be.*

"Your dad paid me what I would've made modeling and took...the baby. You." Her expression did an odd thing, as if a smile was trying to get out but didn't quite make it. "Seems strange saying that after all this time." She scooted her sunglasses up her nose. "Frank wanted the baby himself and that's when things started to cool between us. Didn't want anyone but himself involved in bringing it up."

It. Daisy opened and shut her mouth. There was a term for what Audrey Myerson was doing, where you just stuck to what you knew, even though there was new information that could disprove it. No matter that they were sitting here, mother and daughter, talking face-to-face, she, Daisy, was an *it.*

"The night of the fire, I came over to see him. Like I said, things had cooled but never really fizzled out altogether. After you were born, he'd call and I'd spend the night. You'd be sleeping of course."

Audrey looked out over the harbor. "It got tricky as you got older; he didn't want you seeing me there and he hardly left the house. Then Amelia came back, and it was pretty much over. Except that night he died. She was up seeing a friend in L.A. or something and he asked me to come over. He said you'd be out for the evening."

She smiled. "Turns out he was wrong. We were sitting on his bed, and we heard your footsteps on the stairs. I hid in the closet."

She tapped Daisy's empty glass, then motioned again for the waiter.

"So I was stuck in there between his suit jackets. Hotter than hell—I thought I was gonna die of heat frustration."

Incredibly, given that right now she was literally hanging onto Audrey's every word, Daisy had to fight the urge to correct her. Considering the scenario Audrey was describing though, frustration probably worked.

"Then you and your father get into this big fight, both of you screaming and yelling at each other and he tells you to get out. I remember I was peeking through the gap in the closet, trying to breathe if nothing else, and I saw him point his finger at the door. I waited until I heard the front door slam before I came out."

Daisy absorbed this piece of information. If Audrey was there after she left…"The candle on the windowsill," she said. "Did you notice it?"

Audrey nodded. "I put it there myself, kind of hoping to set a mood, you know. Your dad loved candles."

Daisy nodded, leaning across the table, silently urging Audrey on.

"He was angry when you left, which wasn't good news because I had something that was going to make him a whole lot angrier. Right around the same time he started making this big name for himself with those pictures he painted of you, he did this whole collection of me." She pushed at her sunglasses. "Nudes. Nothing like anything he'd done before, he didn't think much of them, gave the whole lot to me for my birthday one year. Then he started getting to be a name and he wanted them back. I offered to sell them to him." She shrugged. "Like always, I needed money." She shrugged.

"We'd go back and forth like this, went on for a year. He didn't give a damn about the paintings, just didn't want word getting out that he'd done them. He could be kind of a prude sometimes." She shook her head. "I know, go figure. Anyway, I think they embarrassed him. In the end, he kept giving me money to keep my mouth shut. Not just about the paintings, but, you, too. That his darling Daisy was the daughter of some trashy underwear model he'd had an affair with. It was a side of himself he didn't want the world knowing about."

The waiter brought the drinks. "Can I get you ladies something to eat? Appetizers? Would you like to see a menu?"

"We're fine," Daisy said with a glance at Audrey, who had already picked up her drink.

"So the night he died, we were having the same old fight. I needed money, I told him I was going to sell the damn pictures. He started yelling and waving his arms around the way he always did. That's how

I remember the candle. He was up out of bed by then, pacing. We'd both been drinking a little and he tripped over a chair. It hit those wooden window blinds he had in his room and nearly knocked the candle over. I remember I bent to pick it up and he grabbed me by the shoulders and all but hurled me out of the room. He was a strong man, your father."

"And…" Daisy was conscious of sitting very still, hardly breathing even "you didn't go back?"

"No. I could hear him crashing around inside. It sounded like he was throwing things in there. Something hit the door and I decided I'd heard enough. I got out. Next day I saw the news."

"I thought all this time I'd killed my father," Daisy whispered, almost to herself.

Audrey shook her head. "Your father killed himself. It was just the way he lived his life." She finished her drink. "So anyways, it's the same old story. Money to pay the rent, etcetera. I heard this English guy's doing a biography on Frankie and I haven't said anything to him yet, he probably doesn't know I exist. Like I said, we were pretty discreet. Still, I thought maybe he'd like to know you have a mother." She leaned closer. "Or maybe you don't want him to know. In that case, I'd need some incentive to keep my mouth shut."

Daisy stood. "The part where you're wrong is, I *don't* have a mother. Never did. And, quite honestly, I don't care who knows it."

CHAPTER TWENTY

HE'D SPENT THE MORNING down in San Diego doing an interview with an architect for one of the assignments Rod had lined up for him. Heading north again, he found himself stuck in a wall of traffic. It did nothing to dampen Nick's resolve. All the sleepless nights, the breast-beating and saber-rattling, or whatever it was that lovesick swains did, had culminated in a decision. A major decision, and he didn't think that was an overstatement. The driver's window was open, the wind was hot and gusting and on the station of the golden oldies, Neil Diamond was singing.

The traffic had come to a complete standstill and the blonde in the next lane (all right, it might have been Cameron Diaz) looked over at Nick and smirked. *Middle-aged would-be swinger playing Neil Diamond*, the smirk said.

Nick resisted the urge to lean across the passenger seat and ask if she enjoyed Lawrence Welk. Instead, he focused on the new life he had in mind.

A life that included teenaged daughters—one of them only during the summer, but that could change, too—and dogs. Dozens of dogs.

"You make me feel like a guitar strumming," Neil sang.

Nick drummed his fingers on the steering wheel, keeping time to the music. Daisy made him feel that way. *I am not the same man I was when I first arrived in Laguna.*

On the radio, Neil had turned over the mic to Billy Joel, who was singing about his uptown girl, and then a news flash interrupted him. A major, new, wildfire was burning in south Orange County. Nick glanced at the dashboard clock. It was nearly two. He'd just reached the northern end of Camp Pendleton, a sprawling Marine Corps Base and one of the few pieces of open coastline from north of L.A. to the Mexican border. Laguna was in Orange County, he knew that much, but California counties were vast and his knowledge of geography wasn't.

His thoughts drifted back to Daisy. She'd be skeptical, of course; Daisy was skeptical about almost everything. Except animals and hard-luck causes. Now that he thought about it, maybe she was only skeptical about superficial and shallow biographers.

The radio issued another news bulletin. Some homes were in danger and voluntary evacuations were being called for…Static prevented him from hearing more. He punched buttons trying to bring in another station. The traffic was still sluggish, stalling every mile or so. Mixed in with the diesel fumes, he caught a whiff of smoke.

In San Clemente he saw a faint wisp on the horizon up ahead to the north. On an impulse, he pulled off the 405 and took Pacific Coast Highway north. By the time he passed the Beach Shack south of town, where Daisy had told him about Toby, a huge smoke cloud filled the horizon and seemed to be growing by the minute.

He tried to reach Daisy on her mobile phone. She wasn't answering. Getting off the freeway had been a mistake. Traffic filled both lanes north and south, making it pointless to do a quick turnaround and head back to the freeway. Cars inched by fits and starts in a crawl so excruciatingly slow that, as he rounded the bend before the road descended into Laguna proper, he actually considered parking the car on a side street and walking into town.

No faint whiff of smoke now, he could smell and taste it, too. Winds were buffeting the car even at this snail's pace, and the skin on his face was almost crackling. Ahead, the huge cloud of smoke was tinged pink around the base. On the sidewalk, amid the shoppers and strollers who would apparently go about their business until the shops and restaurants actually burned to the ground, a small cluster of people had stopped to look up at the cloud that now almost filled the entire horizon.

"Excuse me." He leaned out the window. "Where is that fire burning, do you know?"

"Up above Laguna Canyon," someone called back. "In the foothills to the north."

"DAD, PLEASE." Emmy was beating on his arm, hitting him so hard she was making the truck swerve. "Just let me out. I won't say anything, I swear."

Toby looked over at her. He'd just pulled onto the 405, and he wanted to get the hell out of Orange County before he had another visit from Officer Friendly like the one he'd had that morning, but Emmy was about to open the door like she'd jump out on the freeway if she had to. One hand still on the wheel, he grabbed her with the other. He'd had a few beers, okay more than a few, but right now the adrenaline was pumping and he knew exactly what he was doing. "You're gonna sit there and shut up," he said. "I don't wanna hear another word about the damn animals or your mom or anything else. When you're a grown-up, you'll understand that sometimes you just gotta do certain things."

"C'MON, EM. Just answer the phone, please," Daisy muttered as she tried to dial Emmy's cell for the third time. "I'm on my way back from Dana Point, sweetie," she said after Emmy's recorded voice had told her to, "Like, kind of leave a message, or something, okay?" "I've got so much to tell you, but the traffic is bumper-to-bumper and I just heard something on the radio about a fire in Laguna and I'm really worried. I know you're okay, but call me as soon as you get this. Okay, sweetie? I love you."

FROM THE ROOF OF Daisy's cabin, where he was hosing everything in reach, Nick could see the massive wall of flames burning just up the hill, so close he could feel the heat on his face, hear the snarling and crackling as it gobbled up everything in its wake. Winds were blowing the fire nearly horizontally across the tops of the hills, where the fire then wound and undulated like a deadly, glowing vermillion snake.

At one point, he'd thought he heard sirens heading closer, but they'd faded off in the opposite direction. He'd arrived to find fire licking at brush just a few yards away from the wooden porch of Daisy's cabin. The goats were out of their pens, all the dogs were running loose. The cabin door was unlocked. Inside he'd found a scene similar to the one in his apartment—this time with the added feature of severed phone lines.

No one was around, but he remembered seeing a poster about an art festival down in Laguna. And with the snarled traffic on the roads, good luck to anyone trying to get back up here.

Hoping to God Daisy and Emmy were both safe somewhere, he'd put out the blaze with the garden hose, then rounded up the animals and shut them in the goats' pen. It had taken him maybe ten minutes at the most but by the time he was through, blowing embers had started another fire at the back of the cabin. From the roof, hose in one hand, he tried to call the fire department on his mobile and got only static.

He stuck the phone in the back pocket of his jeans. Another small fire had started near one of the other cabins, and the air was so thick with smoke and embers he was starting to wheeze. What was it you were supposed to do in these situations? Wet cloths over the mouth and nose? By the time he'd climbed down, the whole place could be up in flames.

Which was going to happen anyway if the cavalry didn't ride in within the next few minutes. The blaze that had started by the other cabin had now spawned another one close to a grove of eucalyptus trees, right next to the pen where he'd secured the animals. He climbed down from the roof and, still spraying water with the hose, ran over to the pen. The dogs greeted him like a messiah, barking and licking his hands, falling all over themselves to get to him. Elvis, in his eagerness to escape, leaped up and locked all four paws around his arm. The goats clearly didn't want to stick around, either.

"Right, you lot—" he muttered as he unlatched the gate "—just follow me and don't argue."

As he started running, he turned around to make sure the animals were all following and saw a wall of flames, as tall as a building, shoot up the ridge then roar toward him like a freight train.

DAISY WAS ALMOST to Laguna before she reached anyone at Emmy's school on the cell phone. "The school was evacuated earlier this afternoon as a precaution," the secretary told her. "But Emily's father came to pick her up around noon. He said there'd been a family emergency."

Daisy hung up and called the police. "My ex-husband has kidnapped our daughter. I don't mean to sound melodramatic, but—"

Someone honked, pulled up beside her and said something about stupid people who use cell phones while they drive.

Daisy gave him the finger. "This is an emergency, jerk."

"Ma'am," the officer said, "I asked whether your husband has joint custody of your daughter?"

"Yes, but…he picked her up from school under false pretenses and he's mentally unstable. I didn't realize that until recently, but…look could you please send someone to look for him?"

She couldn't remember Toby's license plate

number, but she gave them the year and make of the truck and described Toby and what Emmy had been wearing when she went off to school that morning. Her head was pounding—it had been pounding when she'd left Audrey Myerson. Her mother. She couldn't even think about that now, couldn't think about anything except where Toby had taken Emmy.

Half a mile or so before the turnoff to Laguna Canyon Road, she saw the black sky and the curling line of fire up in the hills above the cabin. She didn't even turn off the ignition.

Running and stumbling and crying under her breath, she ran down the hills. Laguna Canyon Road had been blocked off. She pushed herself to the front of the crowd that had formed behind the barricade.

"I have to get up there," she said. "I live…"

And then she saw what everyone else was gaping at.

Nick, surrounded by dogs and goats, coming down the hill, a wall of flames at his back.

CHAPTER TWENTY-ONE

"SHE'LL BE ALL RIGHT, Daisy," Nick kept saying over and over. "Trust me, she'll be all right. Look, drink this." He handed her a mug of tea. "My mother was a firm believer that the world could be set straight with a cup of tea."

Daisy took the mug, wrapping her hands around it. The warmth helped, but her teeth wouldn't stop chattering. In their typically erratic pattern, the winds had changed direction, sending the flames away from the compound. Her cabin had escaped, but the earlier fire had damaged one of the other cabins, which would have to be destroyed.

Thanks to Nick, the dogs and goats were all okay. Freaked, but okay. **Every thought has a consequence.** Emmy would be okay. Was okay. She looked at her cellular phone on the table, willing it to ring. When it didn't, she shot a glance at the house phone. The police had both numbers. Nick, pacing the kitchen, nodded at her mug.

"Drink it, or I shall be forced to punish you."

Despite herself, she smiled.

He shook his head. "This is a very strange woman we have here, ladies and gentlemen. She smiles at the prospect of punishment. Makes one wonder, doesn't it?"

Daisy sipped her tea. He had a dish towel tucked in the belt of his jeans and a preoccupied expression. Dinner tonight, he'd already announced, would be his creation.

The phone rang and she grabbed it.

"Daisy. On the news it says the fires are burning in Laguna—"

"It's okay, Amalia." She bit her lip. "We're all fine. Emmy…is at a friend's house and the animals are fine. Listen, I've got something in the oven, I'll call you right back, okay?" She hung up and looked at Nick. "I know, I know, but if I tell her the truth she'll go to pieces. Besides, Emmy *is* okay."

"That's my girl."

My girl. She held the cup against her chest and sat down at the table. Nick was watching her. He winked. The phone rang.

"Mom?"

THE CALIFORNIA Highway Patrol had found Emily walking along the 405 and returned her to Daisy that evening. Toby had been picked up and arrested later the same night.

Emily was in her room with Kelsey. Daisy could hear their music, hear them laughing as though the traumatic event they'd been through was an everyday occurrence and nothing really to get rattled over. Emmy hadn't wanted to talk about Toby, and Daisy hadn't insisted. She wondered, though, whether the cycle that had started with her own father was destined to continue through her daughter. She vowed that it wouldn't. Tomorrow she would talk to Emmy.

"What I don't quite understand," Nick said from the stove, "is the rationale behind actually browning onions before adding them to the beef. After all, it all ends up mixed together, doesn't it?"

He was wielding a wooden spoon, waving it as he spoke. Daisy took it from him and stuck it back in the pot. She turned down the gas flame.

"Kiss me," she ordered.

"I am ze chef," he said. "I am not to be disturbed when I am creating."

"Tough."

He kissed her and went on kissing her, backing her up against the stove until she could feel the controls against the small of her back. She didn't give a damn. His hand tangled in her hair, his mouth moved to her throat. Her body melted into his and her knees turned to rubber. For a minute they parted to breathe, and then they kissed again.

"Uh-oh," Emmy said.

Daisy pulled away in time to see Emmy, grinning broadly, both thumbs up. "Hey," she called to her daughter. "Get back here."

"She gave us the thumbs-up," Nick told Daisy. "Let's get back to what we were doing."

THE NEXT DAY they drove down to Dolphin Cove to see Amalia. They walked hand-in-hand to the water's edge. The air was cool, bordering on cold. After the hot Santa Ana winds that had spawned the fires, the night had turned gray and overcast. Daisy wore a red parka, and he had on an Aran sweater that Daisy had said made him look like a fisherman.

"I met my mother," Daisy said. "Yesterday."

Nick looked at her. She was facing the ocean, her hair blowing around her face so that he couldn't see her expression. But he'd heard the feigned casualness in her voice. What he wondered was how she'd managed not to mention it until now.

"My God, Daisy. How did that happen?"

She told him. "Weird, huh? I wanted her to be warm and cozy, but she wasn't. Basically, she just wanted money."

He put his arm around her, pulled her to him.

She leaned her head on his shoulder. "You're struck speechless, aren't you?"

"I have to admit it, I am. I don't even know where to start. How do you feel?"

"Okay." She shrugged, her tough Daisy shrug. "I've gone all these years thinking I didn't have a mother, so now I do and she's not the one I would have ordered. Maybe I'll just go on pretending I don't have one."

"Or you could turn her into one of your causes."

"Hey. You know, that's not a bad idea. She's definitely cause material."

He couldn't help himself. "Am I?"

"You?" She laughed. "No, you're definitely not a cause. You're…you. Nick. And I'm going to tell you something…"

"I'm listening."

"Well." She sighed. "Baba says everyone comes into your life for a reason. To teach us some kind of lesson. I thought you were hanging around to write about my father."

"Clearly, that's no longer true."

"I have an idea about that, too," she said. "But first, I just want to say I know the real reason you're here." She held up her fist. "This was me. All crunched up and tight. But now—" she unclasped her fingers "—see? All opened up."

They kept walking, swinging their hands.

"I love you, Nick. It's going to take a long while to sort out all this stuff I've had locked away, but it feels so good to have it out there, instead of moldering away inside. My dad was just my dad. Difficult, combative, contradictory, but also good and kind and tender. Sometimes."

"That's true of us all, really, isn't it?" he said. "Good and bad mixed up together. We do our best within our limitations."

"You're thinking about Bella?"

"Yes. It's funny, I'm here right now because I saw that picture your father painted of you. Something about it captivated me. I felt that if I understood the man who painted it, it would help me understand myself. And although nothing has turned out the way I thought it would, I really do think I've learned some things that will help me be a better father."

Daisy squeezed his hand. "I want to meet Bella."

"You will." They walked on down the beach. Daisy stooped to inspect an unopened clam shell. The damp had made her hair curl wildly around her shoulders. When she looked up to tell him something, her face was animated.

"I wish I could paint," he said. "I would capture you as you look right this minute."

"You don't need paints." She straightened, put her arms around him. "You've already captured me."

Eighteen months later

DAISY WAS IN THE KITCHEN making Wacky cake. No, not because she needed it herself, she'd stopped doing the emotional eating thing, although it was incredibly delicious. Wacky cake happened to be Nick's favorite and she was making it for his birthday. As she stirred the batter, she thought of all the things that had happened in the past eighteen months. Eighteen months, God, that seemed like a long time. Long enough for them to write a book together: *A Portrait of Frank Truman*, as told to Nicholas Wynne by the artist's daughter, Daisy.

The first review came out yesterday, and Daisy had framed it for Nick to see. He'd been living in Laguna full-time for six months now, back and forth between London while they were writing. Bella was over for the summer and she and Emily were getting along just fine. Nick was living in one of the cabins. Typically, he'd insisted on paying rent even though it was the one that had practically burned down and he'd done most of the fix-up. Well, they both had. It was fun. Last night, they'd had a long discussion about building a much bigger cabin for all four of them. Daisy felt warm whenever she thought of it. Actually, she couldn't wait to tell Amalia, who was madly in love with Nick herself. "He is a very handsome and kind man," Amalia had said. "Almost as handsome as your father. But not so—" she'd flapped her hands around, wriggling her fingers "—not so many fireworks."

There are fireworks and fireworks, Daisy had thought. Nick had plenty of the kind she liked.

Toby was on probation. Wildfire was closed. Maybe if he stayed clean, she'd see about giving him another chance. Her mother hadn't contacted her since she'd heard that she and Nick were writing the biography together. Oh, well.

She heard the front door open.

"Check this out." She handed Nick the review, watched the look on his face as he read it. Was this a happy man, or what? They'd written what the reviewer described as the "definitive biography." Well, of course.

"Daisy, Daisy." He shook his head. "What can I say?"

"You just needed me, that's all."

"I did and I do and I always will," he said.

She smiled and put her arms around him, rested her head against his chest, listening to his heart beat and thinking about how much she loved him. *I did and I do and I always will*. Her smile widened. Nick just had this way with words.

CONFESSIONS OF A NOT-SO-DEAD LIBIDO
by Peggy Webb

My husband could see beauty in a mud puddle. Literally. "Look at that, Louise," he'd say after a heavy spring rain. "Have you ever seen so many amazing colors in mud?"

I'd look and see nothing except brown, but he'd pick up a stick and swirl the mud till the colors of the earth emerged, and all of a sudden I'd see the world through his eyes—extraordinary instead of mundane.

Roy was my mirror to life. Four years ago when he died, it cracked wide open, and I've been living a smashed-up, sleepwalking life ever since.

If he were here on this balmy August night I'd be sailing with him instead of baking cheese straws in preparation for Tuesday-night quilting club with Patsy. I'd be striving for sex appeal in Bermuda shorts and bare-toed sandals instead of opting for comfort in walking shoes and a twill skirt with enough elastic around the waist to make allowances for two helpings of lemon-cream pie.

Not that I mind Patsy. Just the opposite. I love her. She's the only person besides Roy who creates wonder wherever she goes. (She creates mayhem, too, but we won't get into that.) She's my mirror now, as well as my compass.

Of course, I have my daughter, Diana, but I refuse to be the kind of mother who defines herself through her children. Besides, she has her own life now, a husband and a baby on the way.

I slide the last cheese straws into the oven and then go into my office and open e-mail.

From: "Miss Sass" <patsyleslie@hotmail.com>
To: "The Lady" <louisejernigan@yahoo.com>
Sent: Tuesday, August 15, 6:00 PM
Subject: Dangerous Tonight
Hey Lady,
I'm feeling dangerous tonight. Hot to trot, if you know what I mean. Or can you even remember? ☺ Look out, bridge club, here I come. I'm liable to end up dancing on the tables instead of bidding three spades. Whose turn is it to drive, anyhow? Mine or thine?
XOXOX
Patsy
P.S. Lord, how did we end up in a club with no men?

This e-mail is typical "Patsy." She's the only

person I know who makes me laugh all the time. I guess that's why I e-mail her about ten times a day. She lives right next door, but e-mail satisfies my urge to be instantly and constantly in touch with her without having to interrupt the flow of my life. Sometimes we even save the good stuff for e-mail.

From: "The Lady" <louisejernigan@yahoo.com>
To: "Miss Sass" <patsyleslie@hotmail.com>
Sent: Tuesday, August 15, 6:10 PM
Subject: Re: Dangerous Tonight
So, what else is new, Miss Sass? You're always dangerous. If you had a weapon, you'd be lethal. ☺
Hugs,
Louise
P.S. What's this about men? I thought you said your libido was dead?

I press Send then wait. Her reply is almost instantaneous.

From: "Miss Sass" <patsyleslie@hotmail.com>
To: "The Lady" <louisejernigan@yahoo.com>
Sent: Tuesday, August 15, 6:12 PM
Subject: Re: Dangerous Tonight
Ha! If I had a *brain* I'd be lethal.

And I said my libido was in hibernation, not DEAD!
Jeez, Louise!!!!!
P

Patsy loves to have the last word, so I shut off
my computer.

* * * * *

*Want to find out what happens to their friendship
when Patsy and Louise both find the perfect man?*

*Don't miss
CONFESSIONS OF A NOT-SO-DEAD LIBIDO
by Peggy Webb,*

*coming to Harlequin NEXT
in November 2006.*

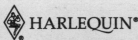

HARLEQUIN®

NeXt™

Entertaining women's fiction for every woman who has wondered "what's next?" in her life.

Receive $1.⁰⁰ off

any Harlequin NEXT™ novel.

Coupon expires March 31, 2007.
Redeemable at participating retail outlets
in the U.S. only. Limit one coupon per customer.

RETAILER: Harlequin Enterprises Ltd. will pay the face value of this coupon plus 8 cents if submitted by customer for this product only. Any other use constitutes fraud. Coupon is nonassignable. Void if taxed, prohibited or restricted by law. Void if copied. Consumer must pay any government taxes. For reimbursement submit coupons and proof of sales to Harlequin Enterprises Ltd., P.O. Box 880478, El Paso, TX 88588-0478, U.S.A. Cash value 1/100 cents. Valid in the U.S. only. ® is a trademark owned and used by the trademark owner and/or its licensee.

5 65373 00076 2 (8100) 0 11266

HNCOUPUS

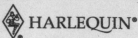

HARLEQUIN®

N_ext™

**Entertaining women's fiction
for every woman who has
wondered "what's next?"
in her life.**

Receive $1.⁰⁰ off

any Harlequin NEXT™ novel.

Coupon expires March 31, 2007.
Redeemable at participating retail outlets
in Canada only. Limit one coupon per customer.

RETAILER: Harlequin Enterprises Ltd. will pay the face value of this coupon plus
10.25¢ if submitted by customer for this product only. Any other use constitutes
fraud. Coupon is nonassignable. Void if taxed, prohibited or restricted by law.
Consumer must pay any government taxes. Void if copied. Nielson Clearing House
customers submit coupons and proof of sales to: Harlequin Enterprises Ltd., P.O.
Box 3000, Saint John, N.B., E2L 4L3. Non-NCH retailer—for reimbursement submit
coupons and proof of sales directly to: Harlequin Enterprises Ltd., Retail Marketing
Department, 225 Duncan Mill Rd., Don Mills, Ontario, M3B 3K9, Canada. Valid in
Canada only. ® is a trademark of Harlequin Enterprises Ltd. Trademarks marked
with ® are registered in the United States and/or other countries.

52607178

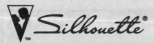

REQUEST YOUR FREE BOOKS!

2 FREE NOVELS PLUS 2 FREE GIFTS!

◆ HARLEQUIN®

Super Romance®

Exciting, emotional, unexpected!

YES! Please send me 2 FREE Harlequin Superromance® novels and my 2 FREE gifts. After receiving them, if I don't wish to receive any more books, I can return the shipping statement marked "cancel." If I don't cancel, I will receive 6 brand-new novels every month and be billed just $4.69 per book in the U.S., or $5.24 per book in Canada, plus 25¢ shipping and handling per book and applicable taxes, if any*. That's a savings of close to 15% off the cover price! I understand that accepting the 2 free books and gifts places me under no obligation to buy anything. I can always return a shipment and cancel at any time. Even if I never buy another book from Harlequin, the two free books and gifts are mine to keep forever.

135 HDN EEX7   336 HDN EEYK

Name _____ (PLEASE PRINT)

Address _____ Apt. _____

City _____ State/Prov. _____ Zip/Postal Code _____

Signature (if under 18, a parent or guardian must sign)

Mail to Harlequin Reader Service®:

IN U.S.A.
P.O. Box 1867
Buffalo, NY
14240-1867

IN CANADA
P.O. Box 609
Fort Erie, Ontario
L2A 5X3

Not valid to current Harlequin Superromance subscribers.

Want to try two free books from another line?
Call 1-800-873-8635 or visit www.morefreebooks.com.

* Terms and prices subject to change without notice. NY residents add applicable sales tax. Canadian residents will be charged applicable provincial taxes and GST. This offer is limited to one order per household. All orders subject to approval. Credit or debit balances in a customer's account(s) may be offset by any other outstanding balance owed by or to the customer. Please allow 4 to 6 weeks for delivery.

HSR06

nocturne™

USA TODAY bestselling author

MAUREEN CHILD

ETERNALLY

He was a guardian. An immortal fighter of evil,
out to destroy a demon, and she was his next
target. He knew joining with her would make
him strong enough to defeat any demon.
But the cost might be losing the woman
who was his true salvation.

On sale November, wherever books are sold.

SAVE UP TO $30! SIGN UP TODAY!

INSIDE *Romance*

The complete guide to your favorite
Harlequin®, Silhouette® and Love Inspired® books.

✓ Newsletter ABSOLUTELY FREE! No purchase necessary.

✓ Valuable coupons for future purchases of Harlequin,
  Silhouette and Love Inspired books in every issue!

✓ Special excerpts & previews in each issue. Learn about all
  the hottest titles before they arrive in stores.

✓ No hassle—mailed directly to your door!

✓ Comes complete with a handy shopping checklist
  so you won't miss out on any titles.

- -

SIGN ME UP TO RECEIVE INSIDE ROMANCE
ABSOLUTELY FREE
(Please print clearly)

Name

Address

City/Town   State/Province   Zip/Postal Code

(098 KKM EJL9)

Please mail this form to:
In the U.S.A.: Inside Romance, P.O. Box 9057, Buffalo, NY 14269-9057
In Canada: Inside Romance, P.O. Box 622, Fort Erie, ON L2A 5X3
OR visit http://www.eHarlequin.com/insideromance

IRNBPA06R   ® and ™ are trademarks owned and used by the trademark owner and/or its licensee.

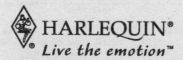